Windswept

Melodi Arentsen

ISBN: 0692821120
ISBN 13: 9780692821121

With deepest appreciation to my darling husband, a magnificent wordsmith--I love you always and forever.

and

With sincere thanks to Kim Marchal, my dear friend and meticulous editor--

Words alone are not enough for either of you.

Elizabeth's Story

1914

Chapter 1

My grandfather said the rain poured the day I was born. He said the clouds were wrung out sponges by the time I had been cleaned up good. He said that was why I didn't cry; the clouds buried the early morning sun, dried up all the tears, and left me with none.

Grandpa's voice filled the cracks and crevices in my mind from the moment I entered this world. Some of the cracks were seeped with truth and love, but there were other places, deep crevices, which were filled with something both intangible and gritty, something I could feel but never quite reach out and hold.

I was but a child and held to his voice like sweet honey, smooth and syrupy. I was born in the springtime when the rains came in torrents, and there was no need to speak because no one could hear you with the wet drops beating on the roof and smashing into the windowpanes. Grandpa said that Katerina, my mother, liked the rain the best.

Grandpa said it was a special blessing that I came during the rain with the sunshine just peeking through the dark clouds, creating an early morning glow that illuminated the new day.

"A clean start!" he said.

Grandma Esther shot herself in the head with Grandpa's old hunting gun around the time I was born, when Momma was just a child herself. Grandpa said it was the saddest thing he ever saw, a woman so caught up in her own darkness that she couldn't walk through its thickness.

Momma never talked about Grandma or the day she spattered the wall of the damp, dark store with her own blood, but Grandpa told the story, long and ragged, over and over again to anyone who would listen. After a while, I was the only one left willing to hear him rattle on about the woman who haunted his mind, long since dead and long since forgotten by everyone else.

Grandpa couldn't forget. Grandma's blood-stained memory hung on the wall of the cluttered, old store, and Grandpa tried to paint over it, but the memory just kept seeping through writing its story there for anyone to read.

"Does no good for a person to hide the past," he'd say. "It'll come back to get you sooner or later whether you can see it or not."

So, the blood on the wall was just as regular to me as the pies Momma made, the candy case on the counter full of Teaberry Gum and King Leo's Pure Peppermint Sticks or the bolts of fabric in shades of blues, greens, reds, and golds stacked high on the corner table. A person just got where she didn't much notice any of it, just took it all for granted it was there.

Not that Grandpa Swanson ever loved Grandma. Anybody would tell you that he never did. Grandma was four years older than my eighteen-year-old Grandpa when they met. It was easy for Grandpa to flatter Grandma, who at twenty-two, was relatively an old maid by some folks' reckoning. She was frumpy and plain, desperate for a man. Grandpa was quite a looker, stocky and strong, with dark eyes and a quiet voice. He was smart, too smart for his own good. According to Grandpa, it didn't take him long to get Grandma up to the hayloft and in love with him.

Grandpa quit coming around after that, but when a couple months passed, and Grandma missed her monthly twice, she told her father what Grandpa had done to her.

The town sheriff, a burly man with a brusque disposition, was called to find Grandpa and haul him into jail for taking advantage of a woman. Grandpa never did take advantage of Grandma, but that's not how she told it. She said Grandpa promised to marry her; they were engaged. Grandpa claimed that he said no such thing. With her word against his, the sheriff was stuck in the middle of a tricky situation.

See, Grandma's father, George Fairweather, had a big, old pile of money. He was a well-respected and, by most accounts, powerful man. A store owner, he held the deed to The Mercantile, the town of Harrisville's only general store. Folks had no other place to purchase their wares, so it garnered much business. George lived with his wife Mathilda and daughter Esther in the nicest house in all of Harrisville. In the eyes of most, George Fairweather was indeed comfortable.

Grandpa's father, on the other hand, had run off when he was a baby, and his mother was long since dead. Grandpa had just been drifting from town to town doing odd jobs when he came into Harrisville. Now he found himself battling the wealthy father of a pregnant spinster.

It had all started when George Fairweather had hired Grandpa to paint a fence on the south side of his property. The fence separated his home from the pasture and beyond that, the woods. Grandma would sashay out to the fence mid-day bringing Grandpa drinks and sandwiches. She would talk to Grandpa of the weather or Sunday morning church services. Grandma loved to talk about Jesus. Grandpa would just smile and tip his hat to her. He didn't say much because he could see George watching them from the window, always keeping an eye on his only daughter.

Grandpa'd say to me, "I knew my goose was as good as cooked."

Grandpa eventually agreed to marry Grandma, and the charges were dropped.

"But I hated her from the first day I took her to my bed; a man's got needs though, you know, especially a young one like me, so I made do with the gal."

Grandma's belly grew larger every day. Grandpa claimed that she was "the ugliest, damn pregnant woman he'd ever seen."

He said, "Esther couldn't help it none that she was getting homelier by the day."

As her face grew round and her body fleshy, she moved very little, talked only of religion, and cooked virtually nothing. She was an irritation to Grandpa, one that he could not escape.

Grandma was beside herself with fear; she knew that the baby would be deformed as punishment for her sinful ways. She just knew that her punishment would be brought forth on this child, and she dwelled on it, day and night.

Grandpa said, "After she growed too big to take care of me, I'd leave at night, go out prowlin', looking to find any woman I shouldn't of been looking for. When I'd come home, Esther would be sitting on the front porch in the middle of the night, just rocking and staring and praying, praying hard. She didn't even know I was there, didn't even know I had been gone. I don't think she even cared if I came back. She was just there, her and the baby in her belly and Jesus, just the three of them, rocking and praying, praying and rocking, all of the time."

As the hour approached for the birthing of the child, Grandma's screams shook the walls in the house and below in the little store filled with coffee, spices, baking powder, milk, and eggs.

Her father had allowed Grandpa and Grandma to live in the little set of rooms above the weathered clapboard store. George had only agreed to this because Matilda, his wife, had insisted.

A small kitchen sat in the back of the store on the same level. Beyond the kitchen was a nook with stairs leading up to the main living area. It wasn't much, but it was more than Grandpa had ever had in his whole life.

In exchange, Grandpa would run The Mercantile. The living space above the house was small, and any noise made upstairs could be heard downstairs, so Grandma's screams echoed through the hall and down the stairs into the store with its shelves full of goods.

Over and over again, she let forth with a voice that sounded of the devil himself. Her whole body shook and shuddered. When the time came to push, she was too spent. The baby wasn't moving. Matilda had been with her the whole time, but when Grandma refused to push, she realized that the baby wasn't coming. The child was stuck. Matilda hollered hysterically for Grandpa, requesting that he bring a knife from the store.

What Matilda thought a boy of sixteen could do, Grandpa said he didn't know, but he went. It was his duty as a husband. What Grandpa saw when he walked in the room that day was his naked wife sprawled out on the bed, her dark brown hair slick and plastered to her scalp with sweat.

Eyes bulging out of her head and writhing, she screamed at him, "Look what the bastard has done to me!"

She said it once, but Grandpa said he heard it over and over in his brain like an echo in a cave. It shook him to the bone, cold to the bone.

"Use that knife," Matilda said.

"Why? Why?" he screamed.

"Because she's going to die if you don't," panted Matilda.

She was a big, bosomy woman with a powerful personality and a demanding nature. Although politeness and etiquette mattered, in times of crisis, Matilda seemed to step forward even more so than her husband, George. She had a take charge personality. In her presence, men faded into the emptiness of the room. Not that she didn't know her place, Matilda knew the role she played; she was a woman. She deferred to her husband, yielded to him at every turn, relied on his generosity to support her. But given the right moment, she would rise up and make her demands known. In this case, she called on Grandpa.

He thought long and hard about picking up that knife from the store. He hesitated, wondering what good could come from it. The room was swirling in slow motion. He saw Matilda tie her daughter's hands to the bedpost. He saw her wipe the blade with alcohol and water. He heard her tell him what to do. He felt the purple skin of Grandma's lower belly and submerged the knife into the surface of her skin, slicing it open. He pulled the baby from her womb and passed it to Matilda. If Grandma was screaming or if the baby was crying, he didn't hear it. There was nothing but silence, empty and cold.

The steaming hot room was spinning faster and faster. Matilda laid the baby, wrapped tightly in blankets, on the bed beside Grandma. He watched her tie off and cut the cord connecting them. Grandpa heard nothing but footfalls on the stairs coming quicker and quicker toward the birthing room.

He watched as a Dr. James Hood, who always wore black from hat to shoes and who looked way more aged than his thirty years on this earth, barreled through the door.

"I came as quickly as I could," he said. "Mrs. Palmer heard the screams and ran to request my assistance." He saw Matilda beginning to stitch the belching stomach.

"Wait," he screamed. "You must remove the afterbirth, and the womb must be sealed. I can suture it. This is her only chance of survival along with the absence of further infection."

Grandma lay still on the bed, gray in the face, a ghost of a mother. Plastered in an alcohol-filled stupor, she was soaked in sweat and looked like death was right around the corner.

Grandpa ran to the child, picked it up in his arms, shook it lightly, and wiped the blood from its face. That child was as good as dead, as good as dead.

His thoughts jumbled in his head. What if the baby died? What if he was trapped forever with Esther and only the memory of a dead baby? He had thought long and hard about being married to Esther. His only hope was the love he might have for his child. Without the baby, there would be nothing left. His future would be empty, without even the slightest wisp of happiness.

Grandpa often claimed, "That babe was the oddest color, a deadly blue pallor."

Suddenly, the child jerked and gasped desperately for air. The baby was alive, born dead but alive. Her breath was ragged but true; the baby would live.

The doctor rose up from his task proclaiming little chance for the new mother's survival.

"A Caesarean birth is a rare event, and in most cases, the mothers cannot survive it. Your only hope is to keep the wound clean and without infection. I will be back to check on her daily until she decides to live or until she decides to die. It's up to that and that alone."

Grandpa explained, "I hoped that she would die right there on that bed because I felt no love for her, but the child, the child clung to my heart like nothing I ever felt before. She clung to my heart because on the day of her birthing, she didn't even cry. That brave little soul just fought for that first breath, took it in, and went to sleep in my arms."

Grandma Esther, however, did cry as she awoke from the stupor of childbirth gone wrong. Upon the doctor's advice, Matilda took to giving her big shots of whiskey to numb her pain.

Grandma had no interest in that baby. Grandpa said he didn't even think she knew that the baby was born; she just lay there whimpering and crying for Grandpa, but he wouldn't come to her, not once.

"I had no love in my heart for Esther," he said.

Of course, with Grandma dwelling in a drunken stupor of pain and potential infection, someone had to take care of that sweet baby, so Grandpa became both momma and papa to her, a baby girl--Katerina, my mother.

The milk from an area farmer's cows gave the baby terrible stomach pain. She would cringe up her little legs, scrunch her face, and open her mouth wide to wail, but no sound came forth, no sound at all, except little gasps of air exhaled in its place. Grandpa tried goat milk, too. Nothing worked, and he watched as his Katerina grew weaker and quieter; she was not thriving, and Grandpa knew it in his bones. His baby girl was going to die while his wife lay upstairs lost in her own selfish pain. She had nothing to give.

"Don't you say I got no heart, Elizabeth," Grandpa would say. "I let Matilda stay in with your grandma and tend to her wounds even though neither one showed any care for my dear Katerina. There was something wrong with Esther, and it had nothing to do with childbirth. I just knew it, and I couldn't make myself go in that room or force that sweet baby's mouth to her cursed breast for fear of catching her disease."

Grandpa proclaimed, "Esther was rotting in that bed; she stunk. It was something sour. Pretty soon, the whole house smelled that way. Every room I tried to live in stunk of your grandmother. She was everywhere; there was no place to hide. It mattered not one bit if I went to her sick room or not. Esther came to me."

Dr. Hood, with a stoic face, made daily visits to check on mother and baby. He called Esther a fighter and said that she would recover physically from the trauma of the birth in good time. The child was declared a fighter as well, but if the mother wouldn't nurse, something needed to be done quickly, or the baby would surely die. A baby unfed could only fight so much before succumbing to starvation.

Word soon spread throughout the town that Nathaniel Swanson was struggling mercilessly with this new babe whose voice was hiding way down in her throat and with his wife who lay in bed lost in the aftermath of childbirth.

Mrs. Adeline Palmer, who according to Grandpa, was the finest looking woman he ever saw, had a generous heart and a nosy nature that could not be quenched with the general Sunday-morning church gossip.

It didn't take her long to gussy up and walk on through the front door of Grandpa's cursed store and home. The floors in the old store were so creaky and worn that a single step could be heard all the way upstairs. But not Adeline Palmer's footsteps. She was so dainty and light on her feet that Grandpa didn't know she was in the store until she was just inches from him.

As she came upon him, Grandpa got a whiff of woman like he had never smelled before in his life, all roses and mint, moisture and powder.

Mrs. Palmer knew everybody's business. Why, she was so sweet and nice, folks just let her in and spilled their lives out on her lap; Adeline got her information directly. What rumor she spread was the plain truth.

Grandpa noticed her plump chest and dewy lips as she began to speak. Adeline told Grandpa something that day that changed him forever. She claimed she knew of a gal who lived in a cabin way off in the woods whose daddy had given her a baby. A sad, sad story she told, and Grandpa said that she told it with such a pink in her cheeks. Her bosom heaving in sympathy for the poor girl, she declared that the baby had been born lifeless and grotesque. The baby was dead from the sins of the father; of course, Mrs. Palmer didn't know them personally, but she was sure that the girl had milk to give. What she claimed Grandpa needed was a wet nurse to take care of his sweet child.

"It weren't meant for a man to do, Mr. Swanson," she said as she delicately tickled herself with her handkerchief.

She thought she could arrange for Grandpa to meet the young girl; maybe money would buy that girl's milk. Mrs.

Palmer's visit was quick, so fast Grandpa thought that maybe she had been an apparition; later, he would say Adeline was an angel for bringing to him the girl whom he loved the most, Lucinda, whose breasts leaked for a lifeless baby.

It was only a few hours later that Grandpa found himself walking down the road headed for the woods carrying Katerina; Grandpa had to do something fast, for his child was starving to death. Grandpa was a desperate man.

His walk to the woods was one of faith in God, babies, and pretty Adeline Palmer. She had said the girl and her father would meet him at the edge of the woods just before the last ray of sun went down on the horizon.

Grandpa arrived early with little Katerina against his chest eagerly searching for nourishment that Grandpa could not provide.

He waited several yards from the edge of the woods. He stood with the child in his arms in the middle of an unplanted field that lay between the garden out back of the store and the darkness of the woods. On the other side of that woods stood the village of High Hill. Grandpa planted himself in the vast space that lay dormant of life, between man and nature.

The father and the girl came walking out of the woods with the sun setting in their faces; the girl's face was lit up in the colors of the sun: pink, orange, red, and yellow. Her hair hung clear down to her waist and loose.

The father walked with a limp and carried himself in a way that showed his ignorance. Grandpa wondered what kind of momma would let this man climb on top of her child. No woman would want this greasy man. As the man drug himself up to Grandpa, he jerked the girl by the elbow. Closer they came with every step, and Grandpa realized that she was hardly a child.

She had to be at least fifteen. Her figure was full and round, her bosom high and full of mother's milk. The sun was in her face, so she could hardly see in front of her. She held her hand up over her eyes to block the light and watch her step. With her other hand, she carried a small canvas bag. It was dragging along the field as she walked bumping and catching on the dried earth. She couldn't have lifted the bag if she had wanted to considering how the man had her in his grips with little opportunity for freedom to walk as she pleased.

Grandpa fought to see her face as little Katerina jostled against his chest. He was walking faster and faster toward her. The father was pulling the girl by the arm all the while. Grandpa started to run; he wanted to see her face, so he held tight to the babe and ran.

He heard no birds, no leaves cascading to the ground, no crackling of squirrels, nothing. The world was silent, and he and the baby and the girl were all who were in it.

He saw her face aglow with the setting sun. It was lightly sprinkled with tiny, dancing freckles. Her eyes, although she barely looked at him, were the fairest shade of hazel. Her full lips parted slightly to reveal a small gap between her front teeth. It was far from a smile, but she was beautiful.

He stopped when he reached the foot of the father who was still dragging the girl beside him.

"You can have her," he said. "She ain't no good to me no more. She is too old. She fights me with all she has got. A man's got needs, don't he, mister? Even a man of the Lord has needs. Take her, but don't you be bringing her back to me when she sasses you once. She's got plenty of milk."

He reached over and squeezed the girl's breast. The milk leaked through her blouse and soaked her; she stared at the grass, ashamed of her womanhood and her father lover.

"Get out of here! Go on!" he said.

The man turned to walk back into the woods; Grandpa looked down at the baby in his arms and the young girl whose long, flowing hair was on fire in the setting sun.

When he looked up again, the man was gone, just disappeared into the dark woods like he had never been there in the first place, like he wasn't ever real. He didn't even take the money Grandpa had brought him. He didn't even ask about it. The man just vanished into the trees.

The girl's eyes fell down upon the child and then raised up to the man, my Grandpa. "She looked right at me with those big brown eyes and spit, Elizabeth. Lucinda spit right into my face."

Chapter 2

*M*omma liked to bake pies; she baked all day long for the fellas who worked in the feed mill down the road. They came into Grandpa's store for thick slices of chocolate custard or lemon meringue; they'd sit on the steps out front of the store every day eating Momma's sweet pies. Without ever knowing her at all, they swallowed every last crumb, and Grandpa was proud of it.

"I don't know how this store would stay in business without those pies, Katerina," Grandpa would say.

Running the store was no easy task. Grandpa could sell only what he could get. Fresh meats, produce, and dry goods could be gathered locally and placed on the shelves. But since a train didn't come through town, Grandpa had to hire men to pick up his wares from the depot twenty miles away.

These wares were purchased from drummers who would pass through on rare occasion. Grandpa could buy soaps, candies, and tobacco from these salesmen, but only when they made it through his doors, so he was right when he claimed that Momma kept the store afloat. This was especially true if he extended credit to his patrons when times were tough, and they often were.

Momma would just look at him with an expressionless mouth. The eyes, however, told the story. They told secrets in your ear, stripped you naked, and placed your heart in your hands. Momma's eyes devoured many a man who walked into the store without her even knowing it herself. Her eyes were the color of warm, summer sand.

On the days Grandpa praised her pies, Momma's eyes filled with shimmering tears that never toppled over the rim, just sat there, balanced between pleasure and pain, teetering. Her reaction to Grandpa always left me wondering just what about pie baking would make a gal feel like crying. Momma seemed to feel pain where it should not have been. Why else would those beautiful eyes glaze over with hurt?

As a child, I got so as I made excuses to get out of Momma's kitchen where I was expected to help with the baking. But there were some weeks when Momma was just too busy with that pie making to let me run free like a child should. I'd spend those days surrounded by sugar, flour, eggs, and butter, but those evenings with no room for supper--I had stuffed my mouth full of Momma's sweet pie dough every chance I got. Momma would just look at me when I did this with narrowed eyes, shake her head, and point her finger at my belly. She'd make one of her scrunched up sad faces, turn, and plunge another pie deep into the oven.

I'd return quickly to the pie dough remains in the bowl, roll it in the sugar, and drop it into my mouth without ever learning my lesson.

To this day, there isn't anything better than raw pie dough to remind me of how sweet Momma was. Sweetness does come with a price to pay, and it was my chore to wipe the counters clean, fill the sink with new water and soap after every pie mixing, and wash up the bowls for the next round.

Momma would make around ten pies a day in the planting and harvesting seasons. My hands were always red and wrinkled by the third pie from all of the washing. I'd hold my hands up to Momma pleading for mercy, a little break. She'd just look at me, put her fingers in the corners of my mouth, turn my face into a smile, and coax me right back to the sink.

A person couldn't escape Momma. She held a person captive with her eyes alone. As a child, I didn't want to disappoint her. It was so easy to see when I had. She couldn't hide it even though she had no voice. I could just feel it, so I tried hard to be dutiful. I didn't want to see that look from Momma, the one that revealed her heartache.

At first, Momma had me stand on an upside down wash bucket next to the sink, so I could reach the water. But by the time I was twelve, I had grown long and had no trouble reaching the steamy water. It was then that I stood without being lifted to do my own work. I had been washing those bowls and spoons and measuring cups since I was five years old. Grandpa said if I was big enough to go to get an education, I was big enough to earn my keep.

The day Momma took the bucket away I knew I was a woman. I didn't have to start my monthlies or wear a corset to know I was grown up. It was the work I did with my hands that whispered my womanhood into my ear. Momma didn't have to say a word. The day the bucket left was the day I began craving that sinkful of dishes. It made me real.

As I washed the dishes, I would daydream of my future. I saw myself with a family of my own, a husband and babies to love. I wanted this most because it was something I had never seen. My family was far from ordinary. I saw other families about town. I would see them walking into church together on Sunday morning. I wanted that for myself, that which seemed normal...traditional. I hoped one day the man of my dreams would sweep me away to our own little home where we would live together with our beautiful children, where we could watch them frolic in the sun, where we could tuck them into bed each night. I wanted for my own children what I did not have for myself.

Momma offered little entertainment when the work was finished, no story-telling or singing danced out of Momma's mouth. So, I took to reading when I wasn't busy with washing and my lessons from Old Lady DuPree who taught me arithmetic, reading, writing, and needlepoint.

I'd search for anything I could find to read: old newspapers that lined boxes, labels on jars and bottles in the store, and the Bible. Of course, Old Lady DuPree thought this reading of mine was a good thing, but there was a battle brewing over what I should be reading. I didn't understand a word of that Bible, but times were hard and coming across another book with so many words was real difficult. Most folks knew the Bible wasn't for pleasure--it was the law. Like I said, I didn't understand that book too much. I hadn't been to church a day in my life. There were just words on its pages; I was desperate for words.

Grandpa always said, "You don't have to go to a church to be holy, but you gotta have a good book out for all to see that you fear the Lord. You gotta place it out for all to see. That's how you get to Heaven's gate. Keep the book out and be afraid what your naughtiness will get you. Ha!"

I'd sit in the back of the store and read that book. Grandpa would make me sit there because it soon spread through town that Grandpa Swanson's grandbaby was setting him right by reading that Bible. Ladies came in by the droves to purchase molasses and coffee and eggs and to see the "Little Disciple" as Grandpa called me.

Now a person might think Grandpa was getting right with his maker, but I knew the old man well. In this old town full of Lutherans, you could strum up a lot of business in the name of religion. Heck, I wasn't reading that Bible to save my soul. I wasn't even reading it to save Grandpa's business; I was read-ing it for the words on the page that filled me up the same way Momma's sweet pie dough filled me. Grandpa didn't care about my reasons; he'd just guide those pursed-lipped ladies by their corseted waists to the milk or cheese or liniment.

You would have thought Momma wouldn't mind my reading out there, but I could feel she didn't like it one bit. She'd stomp out to the store with a dish to be washed. She'd stomp out with a recipe to read. Some days, she'd just stomp out there and stand, white-faced with fire in her eyes.

You see, Momma was sweet, but she was never truly happy. No one would say that about her. They all said it was because my father ran off before I was born. That's what they all said, but Grandpa said the sadness fell on her in the womb. Grandpa said her soul was cursed. That's why Momma was so sad, and that's why she never spoke a word.

Now mind you, Momma could talk though her voice was nothing but air. She could talk love with her eyes and manners with her hand on my bottom. Something was in Momma that a person just knew could never come outside her, something way down deep like water in a well. A person just wanted to take a drink of her, swallow her pain. On Momma, it was beautiful.

It didn't take me too long to figure out that Momma thought I had no business reading that Bible; she thought I had no business at all in that store with the menfolk now that I didn't need my wash bucket. More than that, I was pretty sure she thought Grandpa's stories were not for her baby daughter's ears. Of course, Momma never said it. With Momma, a person just had to feel her.

Momma loved Grandpa. Anyone could tell that, but she didn't want him to know her, to feel her heart. She wanted to stay away from him. The day Grandpa tossed Lucinda out into the street was the day Momma closed her heart to Grandpa. I reckon Momma got so used to the silence between her and Grandpa that it was hard to let go of the saying nothing that comes with being comfortable.

Sometimes, it's just safer to be comfortable. Lucinda always used to say, "It isn't a big thing that your Momma can't speak. It's a tiny thing in this great world. Fact is that most things just aren't worth talking about anyway."

Maybe Lucinda was right, but as a child I'd dream of Momma's voice. It would always be soft and smooth and singing. Sometimes, she'd be rocking me on her lap and humming, cool and drowsy. Other times, I'd see her hanging crisp white sheets on the clothesline outside by the field. She'd be talking to a butterfly, and although I could hear her, I couldn't understand those sweet words. If I took a step toward her, the butterfly would dance away carrying Momma's voice on its wings. I'd always wake up from these dreams a little sad, but just a little because Momma was so beautiful in them.

"Most things just ain't worth talking about anyway," I'd remind myself as I left my dreams, trudged downstairs to the kitchen, and looked Momma right in the eyes.

A person just had to look Momma in the eyes because most times that was where her heart was, and everyone wanted Momma's heart, everyone.

Even when I knew it would make Momma's eyes angry, the words on the pages of that old Bible in Grandpa's store called me to them. By the time I was twelve, I needed words like I needed food. I'd starve without them. Although I thought Momma understood my craving, it was my choice of nourishment that she seemed most unwilling to accept.

One afternoon after Mrs. DuPree's lessons were finished and the dishes all washed, I sneaked into the store, climbed up onto my stool, and opened up to Job. Now Job was quite a fellow, I thought, for the way he played what seemed to be a game of marbles. Job was the Cat's Eye that the Devil and God both wanted in their collections. He was the prize marble that God drew out of his bag time and again to face his toughest opponent.

Well, I was just reading along trying my hardest to sound out some darn hard words. It was especially difficult when Grandpa was standing up at the front of the store with the fellas from the feed mill. They were all just prattling on about how the corn would tassel this year and how they liked or disliked the hot, summer weather, all things that didn't matter for anything. I just got sat down and into Job when Momma came barreling in through the door. She was carrying one large spoon. She stormed right up to me, stared into my face, and snatched that Bible clean off my lap.

I heard Grandpa's footsteps coming. His footfalls were moving faster making the floorboards squeak louder and louder as he approached.

"Get your fanny off that stool here and help me close her up, Elizabeth," Grandpa said with a twinkling eye and a wink at Momma even though she was blazing with rage.

I was not a sassy child, so I grabbed the broom and started sweeping the dusty corners and crevices in a store so stained up that it just wouldn't come clean anymore.

I thought about Momma as I swept. She played the spoon-washing game many times since I started reading that Bible. Why she did it was beyond me. It wasn't like Momma didn't do as a Christian does. Sunday morning didn't include church for us, but that didn't make her any less respectful of the Lord's power. She did unto others as she would have done unto herself. Didn't that make her Christian enough?

Chapter 3

"Elizabeth!" yelled Grandpa. "Are you listening to me?"

"Yes, Grandpa," I said tripping over the broom.

"Now Elizabeth, you know you're not. I was telling you about pretty Miss Lucinda spitting in my face the day her papa drug her out of them woods out back."

I'd heard this one at least ten times before now, but there was no use telling Grandpa that.

He'd just say, "Well, you ain't never heard the way I'm gonna tell it to you today."

But I had--he told all his tales over and over like he was trying to convince himself.

"That gal spit me square in the face." I heard Grandpa ramble as I placed the broom against the wall and climbed up on a stool to sit down.

I figured I might as well sit because this story was going to be a long one, and Grandpa really didn't care if I swept up the store. He was just trying to get me away from Momma and her eyes and that darned spoon.

It had been real hot that day, and the smells of the old store mingled with Momma's supper cooking in the kitchen. It was blowing up a rain, so the air was damp forcing my hair to curl up in ringlets around my face. The sky was turning shades of deep blues and purples. Dust swirled on the road outside the store. Grandpa quickly closed the front door which was often propped open on hot days. He closed it to keep the dust and dirt from coming in. I hated to tell him, but it already had.

"Should've never tossed that gal out the way I did," I heard Grandpa say.

That'd been five years earlier, but I remembered it like it was yesterday. I was just sitting in the kitchen shelling peas with Momma when Lucinda came in. Grandpa was stomping after her. As they approached, their voices were muffled, heated, and angry. I couldn't hear all they were saying, but then Grandpa declared,

"You ain't nothing but a liar!"

I'd never seen him so angry or so loud; I didn't know what he meant. I knew it was bad; I could feel that, but years after, it was just plain unexplainable. Lucinda left that day. Momma cried and cried.

"I brought that girl home for my Katerina, and she took hold of her, brought her up to nurse, and claimed her as her own child," said Grandpa.

The storm was rattling the windowpanes, but Grandpa didn't seem to notice, so I kept on sitting on the wobbly, old stool. I had to be still though because it rocked a little if a person moved too quickly. It would be really easy to end up on the floor. There wasn't any use to move to another stool. Every one of them in the whole store wobbled that way. If my legs had been longer, it wouldn't have been a problem. I'd seen many a farmhand eating pie place his legs down awful quickly to catch his balance on one of these stools.

Grandpa's face broadened into a smile, "I loved that Lucinda, every piece of her. Your grandmother wasn't worth much what with her delirium. I needed a woman in my bed. A man has got certain needs, my child..."

The story Grandpa always told got a little blurry here, but I understood even then that Grandpa had affections for Lucinda like a husband has for his wife. Trouble was Lucinda was no wife, and she wanted no part of Grandpa. There was no doubt about that. Even I knew Lucinda didn't love Grandpa. She was hard-hearted toward him, cold and empty.

"I took to bringing her presents, Elizabeth. She'd be nursing that baby, and oh, she was beautiful. Her hair knotted up loose. Her shoulders were bared with my baby at her breast. I'd bring her peppermint sticks that I had took from the store, make her eyes light up like stars. I'd wait for that smile."

Lucinda had a small gap between her front teeth. Grandpa always said she liked to stick her tongue into it when she was concentrating. It was a small flaw that Grandpa loved best.

Lucinda could be a real devil; peppermint sticks got Grandpa nowhere. He was at Lucinda's mercy. Not that Lucinda had no love to give; she took to Katerina like a wild animal instinctively cares for its young, but for Grandpa, her nourishment ran dry.

"The more she hated me, the more I loved her. I loved her despite your grandmother. I loved that girl. That's all there was to it."

Grandpa's eyes were glazed, and he swallowed hard, "It don't do no damn good to love someone who has too much hatred in her heart to love you back."

Lucinda, according to Grandpa, was nothing but anger, hot and fiery.

"It weren't even like that woman was beautiful. It was something else, like her face was always on burning, like her mind was always moving her along her way, always moving." His voice trailed off as it often did drifting into his own thoughts.

"That Lucinda, when she had something to say, it was said, weren't two ways of looking at it."

He was right. She was always on the move, working her hands, quilting, taking care of us. She'd do her work, just a ranting and a raving the whole time.

Of course, not everybody took her so seriously. Momma and I knew she had a soft heart she was protecting. Grandpa didn't. Sometimes, Grandpa spent so much time talking and trying that he didn't hear Lucinda's love. Oh, but it was there; you just had to listen beyond her words.

A person had to listen to the way Lucinda held a tiny baby, to the way her eyes teared up when she was angry, to the way her arms felt around you when you needed comforting. Lucinda raised Momma and me with a stern voice and soft hands.

Grandpa just couldn't understand that Lucinda wanted no man to touch her.

"I'd come to her and beg and plead, but it didn't do me a bit of good. That woman didn't want me, not at all. Lucinda said I had me a wife and that was that. I didn't have me no wife. I had me a crazy woman."

Grandpa sure seemed right about that considering the stories Lucinda told me and the way Grandma just shot herself right in the head. As a child, I often wondered why a grown woman would choose to die. I wondered if she felt it. I now know she felt it all, every last bit of it. One time, Lucinda spanked my bottom real hard just for tracing the blood splatter on the wall with my finger.

"Don't you be disrespecting her that way."

If she wanted to teach me a lesson, she did.

"Your grandmother was a sick, sick woman. It was no wonder. Having a baby is a cursed blessing, I tell you, a cursed blessing. I know that firsthand, and so does Katerina. You give respect, little girl, for the blood that brought you into this old world, even if it's splattered all over this here wall. It's your blood, too. Do you understand? Do you understand?"

Well, I didn't understand, but lie I did, nodding my head in humble agreement at Lucinda's tirade.

"That Lucinda was a hell of a woman," Grandpa said.

I realized that the storm was slapping beads of water into the windowpanes so hard that they seemed to be quivering.

After supper, Grandpa went out to sit on the old porch connected to the storefront. There were rickety chairs out there that Grandpa set up after his father-in-law, George, passed away and left The Mercantile to Grandma Esther.

George Fairweather hadn't lived much past the birth of Momma. He never came to see the baby nor did he show any interest in the health of his only daughter, Esther. He just stayed up in the bedroom of his big, lonely home that sat on a hill at the edge of the entrance to Harrisville. He stayed there just waiting to die, waiting like he knew he deserved it. When he passed on, Matilda handed the deed to the property over to Grandma.

"The Mercantile is a family business, and a family business it shall stay," Matilda claimed.

But as soon as her husband passed on and she gave the store to her daughter, she hightailed it out of town, headed back to her own kin two states away. She never even said good-bye. She just left her own daughter and my momma with Grandpa and Lucinda. Matilda wanted nothing to do with us, according to Grandpa.

"That woman jumped out of town the first chance she got. The old man kicked the bucket, and she was gone, lickety-split, like she was running from a fire," he said.

Anyway, rickety as the rocking chairs were, there was always somebody sitting in them, a gathering place for neighbors telling tales. But the chairs were likely empty this night what with the rain. Not too many people like to sit out in the rain. Although if Grandpa wanted a cigar, that's where he went, Lucinda's rule. Even though she was gone, it was a habit that didn't die.

I was left in the kitchen to clean up the mess. That was the trouble with being a child, you spent a whole lot of time cleaning up adult messes.

I stepped up to my usual spot at the sink. Momma had heated the water up before supper. It had now cooled. As I began cleaning the plates with the old rag in the lukewarm water, I noticed for the first time that my hands were growing long and lean, working hands, a woman's hands.

I felt the presence of someone behind me; instinctively, I turned. It was Momma. Her eyes were on fire and her face flamed. For a moment, I couldn't tell who was standing there before me, Momma or Lucinda.

Soapy water dripping from my fingers and running down my forearms, I reached instinctively for the book she held out in her hands. Momma did not give me the book; she set it down on the table next to me with tears pouring from her eyes, extinguishing the heat that had engulfed them just seconds before. I could feel Momma, and what I felt was love, bittersweet and aching. She bowed her head and walked out of the room slowly while never once looking for my reaction.

I did not touch the book. I simply turned back to the dishes eager to finish them. I wanted nothing more than to climb the creaky stairs to my room and begin reading the Bible given to me with Momma's blessing.

My room was damp and muggy, and even though a little rain danced in, I opened the window just a bit to let in some clean air. I had placed the book on the corner of my bed as I changed into my gown for the night. I was so thrilled with having a book to read that I cared almost nothing that it brought flames to Momma's face as she handed it to me.

I climbed into bed and pulled myself up on a pillow to read. It was too steamy to cover with even a sheet; I felt exposed, almost naked lying there with the window dripping in the sizzling rain. I could smell the clean coming in the air. The wind died down to nothing but a whisper, the rain slowed to a trickle, and the frogs and crickets began their song.

It was getting late into the evening. Soon Grandpa would drag his feet up the stairs to bed. I could not, however, put that book down. It burned in my fingers and took my breath from me. As with any child, the intensity was greater, for I knew that Momma really felt I had no business with my nose in that big book, but she, like so many mothers before her, gave in to her offspring. I now know that there are some lessons that a parent just can't pass on to a child. They have to be lived to be learned. Whatever the reason for Momma not wanting me to read the Bible, well, I guess she just decided that I would have to figure it out for myself.

I decided to read the Book of Esther like my grandmother. I opened to the right page. I loved the pages of Bible--they felt like onion peelings, thin and sheer, like a veil behind which hid all sorts of hidden treasure.

A worn sliver of torn parchment paper was tucked in the seam of the book. I pulled it out and unfolded its brittle corners carefully.

> *Dearest Esther,*
> *Forgiveness may be hard to find, but pray for it. That*
> *baby will bring you such joy. Accept the child, Esther.*
> *Respectfully,*
> *Your Mother*

Eager to read, I paid little heed to the note. Briefly, I pondered why I had not seen it before.

I devoured the book of Esther but was amazed that I found not a single mention of God in it. I stuck the note back in the book right where I had found it.

As I gently closed the book, I noticed that its cover was slightly more worn and faded. It looked like it had suffered from more use, if only just a bit more. All the same, it was a Bible. I would take what I could get, worn or not.

Chapter 4

*T*hat morning, the sun shone something fierce like it was trying to catch fire to the whole world and burn it up. Steam from the rain blanketed the air, and the flowers were already bent with exhaustion. Some of them in Momma's garden had been pounded into the earth from the downpour as if they were trying to return from where they came to begin life again. It was too late. They were ruined, covered with wet, molding filth.

It was my job that morning to pick up the sticks in the yard left from the storm. Grandpa said, that if nothing else, children were always good to have for picking up sticks, and a person was wise to keep one or two around just to keep from having to bend an aching back.

Besides, Momma could spare me today. It was too hot to eat, especially the sticky, sweet pies that Momma made. Nobody would want to fill himself with sweetness on a biting hot day like this.

Momma rose early this morning and baked but two pies: a chocolate custard and a coconut cream. When I came down the stairs, they were sitting on the counter next to the one slice of chocolate that Momma had cut for my breakfast. I sat down to it, the luxury of a slice of pie already waiting, but when I took my first bite, it stuck in my throat like mud, gagging me. The pie was wasted on me.

When I walked into The Mercantile, Grandpa was standing with Mrs. Teetle in front of the lye soap, "Best soap you'll find, Mrs. Teetle, it will have you squeakin' in no time," giving her a big wink with his whole face and a little nudge to her bloused forearm.

Mrs. Teetle looked hot. Ladies around here didn't dress differently summer to winter, except for maybe a heavy coat or woolen shawl in the snow. Mrs. Teetle was covered from head to toe in dark fabric, layers and layers of it. Her gray hair fiercely drawn up under her bonnet that revealed row upon row of angry sweat beads lined up like quivering soldiers at the base of her neck.

Needless to say, Mrs. Teetle didn't take too kindly to Grandpa's behavior. With a toss of her head and her huge skirt, she couldn't have moved without tossing the skirt, she made her way out the propped-open door without another word--I swear--without even breathing.

Grandpa was just a laughing, "She probably thought I was imagining her naked as a jaybird getting squeaky clean."

I wondered out loud what was so funny about that.

"What's so funny about that? I'll tell you what's funny about that. I was imagining it, that old puckered pickle. What's sad is

I'm getting so old. I can't even get love from an old shriveled up pickle like her. Get on out there now and pick up that yard," he said.

His laughter pushed me right out the door.

Momma's morning glories were rustling on the trellis up against the south fence, and as I built my mounds of sticks, brush, and petals near the burning place, I heard a muffled voice over by the glories as if it were trying hard to tell me something.

The fence, old and stripped of its whitewash, swayed slightly with age. I could not see through the boards, but I knew what lay beyond them--tall blades of grass and the woods from which Lucinda had come. The morning glories were thick and snarled. Momma thought they were beautiful, but Grandpa swore they were the Devil suffocating all life in their path. I saw no harm in Momma's vine. It was strength. You couldn't kill this old fence, but the vine had mounted it all the same.

As I came closer, I realized the vine let forth a single voice, ravenous and melting in the heat. I walked closer, quickly but quietly, so the vine would not hear me approach and stop its magic. It seemed to come from the blooms on the other side of the fence. The voice of the vine beyond the fence grew stronger, beating and pulsating. For a moment, I imagined my grandma praying and rocking on the front porch as she swelled with pregnancy. Somehow, I felt her for the first time, her soul that seemed lost, hiding in the morning glory snarls and tangles, but the voice lay beyond the fence. It was both open and hidden.

The problem stood in looking beyond, if possible, through the rickety fence blocking nature on the other side from view.

I searched slowly, carefully through the tangled ropes looking for a knothole, a crack, anything that would let me see beyond the fence that I faced. My hands were moving through the snarls in search for the light on the other side of the wall. At last, I found a crack in the wood at the base of the fence that had been rotted or pushed out by a small animal trapped in our backyard. I hunkered down low, my bottom up in the air, my chin to the earth, elbows sinking in the vine that was holding me there. I could see a blanket was spread in the tall grass beyond the fence.

Momma lay on her back naked with her arms rising up to the sun. Her hair lay in waves and folds around her face, framing her features and covering her. Through the blades of grass, I saw her rise up, supporting her weight with her arms. When she did, my heart rose to my throat. On the blanket was a man. He, too, wore no clothes in the heat of the morning air. Not a sound came from Momma as he placed his mouth over her breast and drew her up to his embrace. Her back arched as he gave way. His voice had been the vine's ravenous, melodic moans. Momma's head threw itself over and back, side to side. Her eyes gazed over the hole through which I peered into her world uninvited. Someone invisible held me there, forced me to see. Shame rose up in me for the way I felt watching Momma and this man who looked so familiar. Just where had I seen him?

Suddenly, I felt a kick to my bottom, "What you looking at, Little Missy?" I heard Grandpa say.

I rose from the ground, turned to pick up sticks, released from the vines that imprisoned me. I left Grandpa with a silent response to his question as I returned to the chore at hand. I bent down and picked up one stick after another knowing full well he was watching me and wondering for himself exactly what I was looking at beyond the fence.

That afternoon was nothing but steam. It came from every-where...off the top of The Mercantile, on the glass windows of the barber shop across the street, from the folds in the ladies' wilted dresses sashaying down the road, and from Momma's eyes. Every time I looked at her I wondered if she knew. Every time I tried to walk away from her, she was there. Maybe, just maybe, it had nothing to do with what my eyes had seen that morning.

I knew that there was work to be done in the store today, and even though Grandpa hadn't asked me to help, I knew that he expected me to. Funny thing around here, nobody really talked a whole lot about what was expected. A person was just supposed to know that kind of thing. It worked out real well for Momma. She could hold her peace with ease, but today was different. Today, I questioned whether Momma had peace at all.

I walked from the backyard and toward the store's front door. All the while, the hot summer breeze danced across my face, burning my skin.

Katerina's Story

Chapter 1

With no cries did I come into this world and with no cries will I go out. I am Katerina without a voice but with a story to tell all the same. Pulled from my mother's womb, there was no life in me. Somewhere, from above, an angel of God breathed the essence of life into me and gave me a soul. A soul, however, without words.

My mother, Esther, who was ill most of her days, did not raise me. Although I could not speak, I could hear her well. What she spoke was nonsense and gibberish communicated through screams mostly during the night. It was once, however, prophetic and profound. Almost always though, I could hear her through the door to her room where she lay in bed, rambling and ranting. When it was bad, I saw nothing of Lucinda who sat with her during the day until her screaming stopped or until my father came to her room in the evening.

On those days, I turned to my father for a child's needs, which he provided with gentle patience and joy. My father, though terribly flawed, adored me, and I swear on his soul that he did all in his life for me, even before I was born. The stories he

43

could tell, the gentleness of his eyes, his simplicity in all things contradicted the desperation I knew that he must have felt.

Being one with no voice, I expressed my opinions in other ways. As a child, I would pull and tug on the arm that led me where it wanted me to go. I even took to biting for a short time. It worked well, but I soon discovered that it led to Lucinda's hand on my bottom. My father, however, just laughed. So, I learned to speak my desires with my eyes. I knew exactly what look to give in order to get my way, but it only worked if Lucinda was away in the kitchen, and I had my father to myself.

I soon discovered that having no voice could be a real blessing, just by watching others get into all kinds of trouble with the words they spoke. I learned that my mind was quiet, and my thoughts were clear. I was always inside of myself. Speaking without thinking first was never a problem for me. I had more time to think and more time to feel, not just myself but others as well. People talked all the time, but what they said was not what they felt. I was convinced that the more people talked--the less that they really knew themselves. I felt no sadness for my affliction.

Of course, my father sought treatment for me from Dr. Hood, but there was none to give. My hearing was fine; it was not hard to learn the language. Lucinda taught me. She would hold up an object and say what it was. I learned quickly by storing pictures in my mind. Lucinda also taught me to read and to write. These, as well, were not difficult because my hearing was acute, so I had as much schooling as a regular girl my age, but anyone who knew me realized I was far from regular.

I chose for myself what others would not choose. Lucinda told me that I had been given a gift. I decided that if God had intended for me to express myself to others with words, he would have given me a voice. I chose not to write notes to others to express myself. I saw what words did to people. I felt the reactions in others. I knew that this was not my path.

There was gentleness in my eyes and a clear steadiness, too. Lucinda said that I was wise beyond my years. Funny, I thought that she was. My father, being a big talker, really didn't protest my decision to communicate this way. I enjoyed his stories. He loved to talk, and I loved him. Avoiding the note writing gave my father the freedom to speak to me without encumbrance. There was no slowing down. I listened to him, and he knew me well enough to understand my expressions--my eyes told all.

My childhood passed as simply as any other childhood, except for the mother who hid beyond the bedroom door. This door lay at the end of the long hallway upstairs. If a person knew no better, one might think the door led to an attic. It was never open, and the light around it was peculiar. It was quite dark toward the end of the hall, but the door was always visible. It was never hidden and always beckoning. You couldn't walk down the hall without acknowledging it, and that was so frightening. I wanted nothing to do with what lay beyond the door, yet it pulled me toward it all the time with a force difficult to resist.

I saw her infrequently and learned to accept it like any other thing children allow to pass by them even though the door tugged at a dark curiosity within me. My father never really spoke of her. He said I should just pretend that Lucinda was my mother, and so I did without too much trouble at all. I was, of course, merely a child.

Lucinda was power. She, too, adored me, but in a different way from my father. I think she adored me for my core of solitude, how in some way I had allowed only what I truly wanted to penetrate my feelings. She, for all her tirades, seemed quite heartbroken like someone had lifted her soul out of her chest and put it back again--tainted.

Tainted or not, she took care of my mother as if she had always known her, had always loved her. Her adoration of my mother was so strong that if a person didn't know any better, you would have thought they came from the same womb. It was like their souls were connected. I think Lucinda felt my mother's pain in a way that, as a child, I just could not comprehend. Wise as I was for my years, I gave little consideration to the pain my mother felt. I held tightly to the selfish ways of a child. Lucinda didn't have to consider it; she really felt it deep inside her like a wound that just kept festering. The more my father begged Lucinda for her affections, the more she served my mother.

Why Lucinda couldn't love my father was a mystery to me. I loved him. Who wouldn't love a man who adored every breath taken by his daughter, whose smile and laughter filled the room with warmth? I saw the man who raised me through the rose-colored glasses of youth. As a result, his hatred of my mother rubbed off on me in ways that children don't even consider. She embarrassed me with her ranting, the strange noises that she would make in the middle of the night haunted my dreams. At the age of nine, I took to sleeping at the foot of Lucinda's bed for the entire summer because I feared that my mother was really a ghost sent to frighten us. A woman as crazy as that couldn't be a real person. There wasn't a person in our house who didn't feel haunted by my mother, who didn't fear her. That wasn't even something that I needed to worry about speaking.

Mother was surrounded by darkness. It seeped through her pores and sucked the life out of anyone who entered her room even for a minute to bring a tray, to make sure she hadn't harmed herself when the screaming was over, whatever the reason. I avoided that room. I avoided my mother's threshold, the end of the long hallway, all of it.

Chapter 2

A person could easily shrug off the effects that a parent has on one's childhood. I could. But the truth was that Lucinda was not my real mother.

She knew she wasn't, but my father just liked to pretend that she was. Nothing was true in the house where I lived. It was all lies. Because I couldn't talk, I saw and felt more. I had hunches, thoughts that just wouldn't leave my heart. Of course, I didn't express them with my voice, but I tried to show them with a gentle touch or glance. I learned that I could communicate more with my eyes than most people could ever say with a million words at their disposal. I wasn't angry at the charade that went on all around me. Instead I danced through it realizing that it was done with love, mostly for me.

Lucinda did not love my father. She loved me and my mother, and that was why she didn't leave. That was why she tolerated his advances, put up with the role she had to play to stay with us. When she couldn't take it anymore, she would cry with rage, tears that just rolled down her flushed cheeks.

You see, Lucinda felt that my father didn't do right by my mother, that he turned his back on her, that if he had just loved her, my mother would have recovered from the stupor of childbirth. Some nights, when my father worked after supper, she would sit at the table for hours with a bottle of whiskey taking shot after shot. She giggled at first at the way it burned down her throat and into her stomach. She loved the way it seemed to set her on fire. It was on these nights that she would sit at the table and pour out her heart to me. She would tell me her truths as if I were her dearest friend, not merely a child. I guess that Lucinda was drunk, but she never seemed that way at the time, only free.

She told me stories of her momma's eye and Manchester. Not once did she call him her father. She hated all men deep within her soul. This hatred took root in her and affected every step that she took in her life. To me, it kept her from the love of a good man. To her, I can now see, through the eyes of womanhood, it kept her strong.

I had images of my mother embedded in my soul. I remembered her walking down the hallway in the wee hours of the morning. She was wearing a white, flowing gown, and she was chanting. I don't really remember what she was saying. It was so muffled, so smothered by other things I couldn't touch. She was shaking her head and pulling her hair as if possessed by some great demon that would not release her.

Once, as I sat on the edge of the steps, I heard her step out of her bed and walk across the floor. Such a panic rose in me that I felt my heart beating, pounding in my head. I wanted to cry out for Lucinda, but no voice came forth. I heard my mother whisper my name through a small crack that she made in her bedroom door. She began to sing my name as if I were a babe in her arms. I ran downstairs as fast as I could. I felt her image behind me, chasing me all the way through the kitchen and into the store. When I turned around, she was not there, as always.

My father told me the story of my mother time and time again, and it was always the same. It never faltered in its plot, nor did his emotions waver. He was as consistent as the sun rising every day, whether a person could see it or not.

Lucinda, however, had a different opinion. She claimed that, way down deep, my father was lying. "All the way through his teeth," she would say with a grittiness that would take me hours to wash from my thoughts. The older I got, the more tired I grew of this game. Of course, Lucinda didn't see the merit of my father's lies, didn't recognize that he may have good reason for it. In her book, a lie was a lie. All lies were dirty.

Because I had no voice, I listened closely to what everyone said. As a child, I would listen to Old Lady DuPree chatting about her latest suitor with the women on the front porch of The Mercantile.

"He's quite young, quite charming," she'd say.

The problem was that Old Lady DuPree was just that--she was old. All suitors, and they were few and far between if at all, were "young and quite charming," but they never materialized, never walked into the store with her on their arms.

A person could say that Old Lady DuPree was a liar, but who was to say? In her mind, these men might exist. In that case, she wasn't lying at all. Just because the regular person of the town couldn't see suitors at her door didn't mean that Old Lady DuPree couldn't see them. Possibly she made them up to allow her an interesting conversation or to be viewed as lovable. In general, humanity has its reasons for lying, and they aren't all bad reasons either.

Chapter 3

At the age of fourteen, I knew I was beautiful. I just knew it. My hair hung long, way down past my waist. It was dark chestnut. My eyelashes were thick, and my face glowed with youthful light. For a young lady of no voice, I was quite vain, even though I saw in others where vanity led to misperceptions.

My body began to develop. My hips grew full and round, my waist narrowed, and my breasts filled the blouses that I adorned with fancy buttons and ribbons. Lucinda warned me not to draw attention to myself in that way, but I felt a heat rising in me, a sensuality that shamed me but frequently empowered me, too.

It was at this age that I transplanted a wild morning glory from the fence posts out beyond the backyard of the store. To find the morning glory, I trudged out around our own backyard fence and into the field that separated The Mercantile from the woods. The morning glory was in full bloom about halfway to the woods. It had captured a piece of fence that held back roaming cows to the east of the field itself.

I brought it into our garden, and it forcefully climbed up, over, and around the whitewash fence that blocked our house from the woods where Lucinda had come. I tended to this vine every day, amazed at its power to regenerate itself and to take over and suffocate all life in its path. My father said it was a weed, nothing more than a murderer of roses, but I saw something wild and free in it, something that would only endure.

One hot summer day, I walked out to the garden only to see that my father had chopped it down and ripped it out by the root. I was instantly enraged. My heart was on fire, so I walked into the store to confront him. I looked him directly in the eye even though The Mercantile was full of men, dirty men whose bodies smelled of work and sweat from laboring on farms and in fields. I didn't have to speak, didn't have to say the words that I would not have been able to produce anyway. I stared at him. I shed not a single tear, just refused to look away from him. I held his gaze, not allowing it to escape. He knew. It burned a hole inside of him. I could feel him. He knew he had done wrong.

The morning glory was mine. I alone had the right to determine its fate. I could choose to water it, to allow it to thrive. But I could also choose to deprive it of life. Either way, it was my decision, and not his, to make.

He had uprooted me, just like he had uprooted my mother and Lucinda. I had a chill in my bones on a day near the temperature of Hell, not because he meant me harm, but because he thought that was what he had to do.

For the first time, I saw how a man could just rip out a woman's strength all in the name of what was his and what he decided was right or wrong. The morning glory was mine. I knew that I would have to face my mother and her truths.

As my father's eyes welled with tears, I turned slowly and walked defiantly away from him. I would always love my father, but it was never the same, never without doubt or fear of his potential.

The morning glory could not be killed, and within just a few days, it burst forth through the damp earth once again. For years, he tried to pull it up, to rip out its soul because he believed that it was something more than it was. To me, it was a symbol of the strength to endure. To him, it was a nuisance that he could not destroy. His attempts at its destruction, though, had marred my heart.

Chapter 4

$\mathcal{L}$ucinda told me that my mother wasn't really crazy, just horribly sad. Although I wanted to believe her, doubt sat on my brain like sludge day after day considering what my father had always said. I had never stepped into that room. Why, just the thought of it made my stomach turn, but Lucinda supported my decision to enter her room even though my father pleaded for me to stay away.

"You'll be full of her stench, Kat."

I figured that I was a strong enough woman to handle the encounter. I tried to reassure my father of my love for him with a simple glance or a gentle touch to his arm. I felt his greatest fear: the loss of my love. I believed that if I could pacify my father, then I could surely figure out how to handle the woman hiding in that room.

I found myself blooming into womanhood and turning toward Lucinda for guidance. She, of course, knew that I would have to confront my mother some day soon, yet she stood by my indecision and my fear, working through it with me. All the while, my mother's tirades increased. Louder and louder did she scream each night. She began throwing things around in the room. After she calmed herself, she spent hours just knocking on the walls in the room. Little tiny knocks echoed down the hallway and into our rooms like she was trying to find a secret passageway into another world or a soft spot that would give her room to breathe. The knocking often came in the wee hours before dawn. Lucinda would go to her then, and I could hear her talking to my mother, sometimes laughing, sometimes not, but always talking.

Lucinda said they spoke of all things, but mostly of what was true in this world because the truth was all that my mother shared with this place. Lucinda and my mother had that in common.

My father's image began to fade at this time deep into the recesses of my mind, never without love but always with questions. Lucinda said that my mother had a story of her own to tell, and since no two stories were ever alike, she claimed that my mother's story deserved to be heard. She told me that it was time to step through the doorway, to take a chance that there was something more to be felt.

What worried me most was that my mother wouldn't accept my missing voice. I thought that in some way it might send her into a fit of madness when I couldn't respond to her or talk to her the way Lucinda always did. I drummed up the courage from a place of strength deep within my soul. This place was gnarled and tangled, but it persevered. It led me down the hall to the door of my mother's bedroom.

I remember the rain pouring down and running like a wild river off the top of the roof of the house. I could hear the torrent bashing into the windowsills. Lucinda offered to come with me into the room, but I did not want her there. I think that was why it took me so long to enter my mother's world. I had to walk into it alone. If my father had not ripped down the morning glory, I was not sure if I ever would have felt how truly alone most people were in this world. Those closest to you could not always be counted on to do what you wished. That was not to say that my father didn't do me a favor that day. He did. He showed me that we were not here for our desires but for our spirits, whether the lesson hurts our hearts or not. His actions placed the truth in my hands. I since realized that some of my greatest life lessons came disguised as anger and hurt. Only those who felt pain sought truth and goodness.

Chapter 5

With the rain pouring down, I stepped through that door and started down a new path in my life. My mother lay on the bed. I could tell that Lucinda had taken extra care to make her look beautiful on this day of all days. She wore a white gown as always, but this one had a thin pink ribbon running around the collar. It tied in a bow at the base of my mother's neck. She was propped up high on pillows, and her eyes were closed. She looked ragged and angelic all at the same time, and in a moment's passing, I knew she was not the demon of my childhood, not a spirit or ghost. She was my mother.

People placed walls between themselves and others, protection from hurts inflicted by others. My mother's madness was one such wall, I was sure of it.

The room was filled with sparse decorations such as tiny dried flowers and a child's delicate pair of white Easter gloves, yellowed with time. These lay on a small chest of drawers next to the one tiny window. A billowy curtain covered this same window allowing only a bit of daylight to enter. On the wall above my mother's bed was a cross. A weathered Bible sat on a table beside the bed. Next to the Bible was a small washing bowl and pitcher of water.

Although mother's face was ashen from lack of fresh air and sunlight, her cheeks appeared warm and rosy like she was a young girl who had pinched them before meeting her suitor. I found this especially peculiar. She seemed like a child lying there in that bed. I wondered if people who never really lived their lives ever aged. My mother had been hiding in this room for as long as I could remember; fourteen years had passed since she had stepped outside of this house. Fourteen years seemed like eternity to me.

I stepped up to her bed and waited for my presence to wake her. I was afraid to touch her, to send her into some fit if she didn't recognize me. Minutes passed before she stirred, opening her eyes to her baby daughter before her who was now a young woman. She looked me straight in the eyes. There was no fear, no judgment; there was only love. Without saying a single word, she had spoken to me. I was not afraid of her or of what was to come.

With shaking hands, she reached for the Bible and placed it on her lap. She opened it to Esther.

She spoke with such dignity, "That is my name. Your mother's name is Esther, but your father's name--it is not Nathaniel."

I looked at her with intensity trying to digest this new reality.

"Surely, Nathaniel loves you very much, but he is not what he appears to be. We have sinned against him, creating a desperate man, doomed by the path we forced him to walk. It was because of our shame that I lay in this bed day after day. I cannot face the light…I cannot face what is unforgivable."

If there was any time in my life when I would have wished for words, it would have been this moment, but there were none to give.

"You carry our shame every day. You were born without voice to pay for Father's sins. You cannot speak our shame. You must carry it, and what a heavy burden…My pain for your soul weighs heavy on my heart. I am filled with rage at a father long since dead, a sick and twisted man."

I wanted to tell my mother that I did not understand, that I didn't see my silence as a burden. I wanted to tell her a million different things.

"By day, I am at peace for the most part, my dear, but at night, my father haunts me, rips out my heart over and over again, denies me my happiness. I have prayed for this day. I prayed that when you came to me that you would be able to carry the weight of our truth. I fear that my time to pass on to you what is real is very short. I worry that I will not meet you one day in Heaven. I will drop into the netherworld of demons who could not overcome the evil before them on earth. I allowed the devil to suckle at my breast and fill me with his own blood. I have sinned unforgivably. Father was the devil who took advantage of my innocence and bribed me with my own shame. He took my virginity. I could not give it to another man."

She went on, "He knew that I was with child, and he knew the child was his. I had already missed my monthly before I lay with Nathaniel in the hayloft. My father made it look like Nathaniel had done wrong by me when, in reality, it was he who had sinned. You are the result of terrible sin, and because of this my dear, sweet Katerina, you have been stripped of your voice. The truth will not be yours to tell, but the sin will be yours to carry. I know that passing this burden to you means that you have to hold the sorrow in your heart. My hope is that some day the story will be told, and that the truth will reveal itself." She stared intently at the wall across from her bed.

"Nathaniel does not know. He believes that you are his, but the hatred he feels toward me betrays what his soul feels. He knows the truth way down deep in a place that he cannot reach. I will never tell him. I am a weak woman with too much fear to face what I have done. The pleasures that my father gave to my body cannot be forgiven. I allowed myself to feel the release of his body into mine. I waited for him to come to me, and I begged him not to send me away to Nathaniel. I couldn't bear to live without his love. This is the evil that your mother is, Katerina."

With that, she handed me the book that lay open on her lap. I felt as if God were not present in the room, as if the Bible were actually the devil's words, like when my mother read it, the letters formed other words with other meanings. When I looked at the book, the words on the page were the same as always, but the weight of it felt heavy in my hands.

I opened the cover of the old Bible and read the inscription on the first page:

To My Darling Esther on your Birthday
August 7, 1878

George Fairweather's handwriting was clear and youthful. I imagined him a smartly dressed man with slick, dark hair and spectacles. The back of the book was filled with some scrawled journal entries written on the onion skin-like pages. These were not George's words. No, they seemed to be written by Esther herself.

I looked up from the book to see her staring at me intently, "I am giving you this book so that you may know what is true and look to it in all things. Do not be distracted by what is unreal; instead, you must turn in the direction that life's path leads you. This path you are walking is not one of falsehoods. Let the truth be known whatever that cost may be."

With that, I walked slowly toward the door. Holding the heavy Bible in my hands and feeling it burn through my fingers, I knew her eyes were on me, but I did not turn to meet her gaze. One shaky hand reached out for the door. I opened it and walked out, closing it quiety behind me. In a daze of shocked thought, I walked in a trance down the hall and into my own room. I sat on the edge of my bed and opened the book, not to read God's word but instead to read my mother's. I knew I had been handed the truth.

Chapter 6

August 7, 1878

    oday Daddy gave me this Bible for my sixteenth birthday. Momma said I could write on the empty pages in the back of the book. I am becoming a woman, and Momma believes that it is time for me to marry. I look toward the day when I will greet a suitor in the parlor. I will wear my best dress and pinch my cheeks to bring them to blushing when he walks in the room. And one day, I shall be a most adoring wife. Momma says that I cook and sew with great skill, both abilities will make me attractive to a husband. Daddy says I need only to smile, for my face lights the room like sunshine. Besides, we come from good stock with plenty of money; he sees no reason for me to labor. A gentleman will find me, a true gentleman. Daddy looks to me like I am a woman now with his glassy eyes. I believe he truly sees me as a beauty.

    Momma says, "Pretty is as pretty does." I know Momma's eyes don't hold the stars for me that Daddy's do. I have earned the sturdy features of Momma's side of the family, a broad nose and full mouth, but my eyes are soft. I brush my hair every night till it shines. It is long and thick. Daddy likes me to wear it down all the time though Momma feels it is not proper. She says a distinguished young lady must appear neat and poised, not loose and aflutter, so I wear my hair up most days. Tomorrow is Saturday, and I will wear it down, for Daddy has promised to take me with him to the store. I am sixteen now. I may help him there.

August 8, 1878

Daddy and I spent the day working together at the store much to Momma's disgust. She believes that a young lady should spend her days doing finer things: piano playing, crocheting, and baking. Momma's will is not as strong as Daddy's which is how Daddy says it should be.

"A wife's opinion need not be heard," he always says holding his finger to his lips when Momma protests this thing or that.

I love Daddy, but my husband will want to hear my voice. I just know it because Daddy wants to hear me, although he seems to have no use for Momma's pursed-up prudishness.

Daddy says I am getting quite a womanly shape. He brought home some fabric from the store for Momma to sew me a courting dress. I wish that he would have let me pick the color, but he is set on pink with little checks.

Daddy grazed my breast today with his forearm as we passed behind the counter. A strange feeling shot up through me. I did not say anything to him about the accident. He looked at me and smiled. I smiled back.

August 10, 1878

What a beautiful Sunday we had. We rose early for church and Momma fixed a big dinner. I entertained Daddy in the parlor with my piano. We sang all afternoon, me and Daddy and Momma, the Fairweather family all together. They say Mrs. Brefield's son from High Hill has requested to call on me next Saturday afternoon. Daddy does not seem pleased with him. He says he is too common for his little girl. Momma says the Brefields are good people with a lot of land. His name is Thomas. It is a strong name, but Daddy says he knew someone named Thomas once. He couldn't be trusted, had shifty eyes. Momma spent today cutting out and piecing together my pink checked dress although Daddy swears he won't let me wear it for a boy named "Thomas."

I was, on the other hand, quite bored today. My schooling has stopped since I have come of marrying age. Momma says I am blessed to have been educated so well. Tomorrow, Daddy says that I may return to the store with him. Someone is knocking at my door.

August 11, 1878
Daddy is having one of his spells today, and we shall not open the store. I worry that Daddy is not all that well. Last night, he came to my bedroom door and entered my room. He hasn't done that since I got my monthlies. Momma says it isn't proper. But, last night, he came knocking. He said he needed someone to listen, that he was worried Momma was touched. I told him I didn't know what he meant. He said he thought she was losing her mind. Daddy scared me; Momma doesn't seem to be losing her mind to me. She is just particular and proper.

I told Daddy not to worry, but today, he has spent the entire morning in bed. The light hurts his eyes, so Momma has kept the shades pulled tight, even though the day is beautiful, and the fresh air and sunlight would probably really do him some good. I am sure he is just worried about Momma, but he was quite peculiar last night. He leaned in to kiss me before he left my room. Tears were streaming down his face, for he said that Momma had rejected his affection. I turned my head to give him my cheek, but he gently grabbed my chin and lifted my lips to his. His tongue stroked like a feather across my upper lip. I pulled back in shock. I have never felt such a thing; it sent chills through me, and although the sensation was sweet, it felt unclean. When he left the room, I felt the tightness and ache in my breast like I felt Saturday in the store. I felt like a child and a woman. Was it proper for a father to kiss his daughter in such a way? I think Momma would not find it so. I will say nothing to her. Daddy is worried for her health, and I am sure that this kiss was nothing. Besides, I fear it will anger Daddy if I speak of this.

August 14, 1878

My dress is finished, but I haven't written of it being so flustered by Daddy's strange moods and the arrival of my first suitor tomorrow. At some point, I guess I should read the Bible, too, but I am fascinated by the feel of writing on this fine, thin paper. There is something in the way the ink glides onto it and scratches each page. I dare say I will not start reading until the empty spaces are filled with my own words.

Mr. Thomas Brefield will arrive here tomorrow afternoon. I, according to Momma, shall wait in the parlor while she greets him at the front door. Momma believes that a mother should always get the first look at a daughter's suitor. The store has been closed now for the fourth day. Momma is worried sick about Daddy. He refuses to get out of bed and has grown quite rumpled lying there all this time. He says he is sick, so we must believe him, but I confess that I see nothing wrong with him that a little soap and some good nourishment would not cure. Momma has been working so hard around here while Daddy has been sick in bed. She wants everything to be perfect for Thomas's arrival. There are fresh flowers in the parlor and at the front door, and in the last few hours, she has made me try on my dress three different times to make sure it is cinched properly and that every seam is secure. It is a beautiful dress, and I do hope Daddy will rise tomorrow to see me in it.

With Daddy in bed this week, I spent much time alone with Momma who seems her normal self to me. It is Daddy I worry about most. He is so odd, so peculiar. Many times, I have pondered whether or not to tell Momma about his kiss. The words do not come, so I hold that strange moment within my own thoughts. Daddy loves me. He will get better. I am sure.

August 15, 1878

It is early morning; he has just left my room. I dare not say to anyone what I am about to write, so I place it here in this journal. He entered my room when the moon was still high in my windowsill. He frightened me, for I was sleeping. He spoke nothing but hovered over my bed for what seemed an hour. I did not move; it was all too strange; he was strange. He seemed to be some other person. It was quite dark, so I spent much time struggling to peek from the corner of a sleeping eye to see him. I thought, at first, that it was an intruder come to steal me away from here. I could not move. My heart beat high and strong in my head. It pulsated in my ears and drowned out any noise or rational thought in the room. Shortly though, the beating slowed, and I thought all was quite possibly just a dream, that truly no one was there. I was wrong, Daddy was in my room. I opened my eyes to look up to him, to ask him why he was here. He placed a finger to his lips and climbed in bed beside me.

He turned me on my side and nestled up behind me. I could feel his body pressed against mine, and I felt a kaleidoscope of emotions, uncontrolled and discomforted. He jerked my nightdress up high around my waist. My legs were bare. I wanted to cry out, but I was afraid of him. What would he do? Would Momma be mad at me? Would he be mad at me? I lay very still and pretended to be sleeping. I could feel the heat of my father up against my buttocks. I heard him rustling with his own pajama pants and suddenly felt my father's skin against mine. My father lay against me. I felt him writhing, pushing against me. I started to scream, but he placed his hand over my mouth. I felt wetness paint my buttocks and spine. I was too frightened to move. I lay still, hardly breathing. My father's breath grew shallow, and I knew he was falling into sleep. Still, I did not move. I didn't do anything.

I have to hurry, for Thomas will be here shortly. I do fear that I will look quite the mess, my eyes puffy from crying. I cannot concentrate any longer. I dare not say anything, for Daddy loves me. Surely, I am upset over nothing. He loves me, I know he does. I must hurry. Thomas is coming.

August 15, 1878
Thomas has gone, and I am in a fit of sadness because of Daddy. Thomas arrived promptly and brought with him a large bouquet from his mother's garden, bright-colored asters and others with heads as big as plates. They were beautiful, and it was dear that Momma was quite taken with the young man, and so was I. Unfortunately, Daddy descended the staircase shortly before tea was served and promptly denounced the bouquet. He said it was too forward and completely improper for a young man to bring

flowers such as these to a girl he hardly knows, and he proceeded to escort him to the door.

I said that they were quite lovely and to come closer and smell them. Momma, then, pronounced them completely charming. To which Daddy replied that the female gender should do so well as to remain silent in the presence of gentlemen. My beautiful pink dress was wasted, and all because he is behaving so strangely. After he had expelled Thomas from our house and returned himself to bed, I spoke of this to Momma. She quieted me with her eyes. I saw the utter lack of acceptance in them which did nothing but irritate my dreadful stomach.

I am not sure how to approach Daddy anymore. He has become something different. He's changed. I can turn to him with love, but I fear something peculiar will happen again. I feel it, and it is wrong. Love and pain mix together. I don't know what I am to do.

Chapter 7

This was all that was written in the Bible my mother gave me. The rest of the pages were filled with the Lord's word, but I knew what I needed to know. My mother and her father were unclean. I was the outcome of this. I was flawed by this horrible union of sins. I was not Nathaniel's child. My heart shattered. Surely, Lucinda and my father knew? Everything I once recognized as truth came tumbling down on my mind and lay in shreds at the bottom of my soul. I was no longer the person I believed myself to be.

I continued my days in silence as it was not my choice. I reflected on what I had learned from my mother...It haunted me...I read it again and again. I showed what was in the Bible to no one but secretly wondered if I were actually hiding anything. My father and Lucinda spent time with my mother in that room every single day. Had she also shared her truth with them? Even though she appeared lucid when speaking to me, the reality was that she was normally anything but. She could have said any of these same things to either or them. My mind spun around and around weaving quite a tangled web, and it was spun from the tales of others. Which tales were reality seemed indistinguishable and to sort out the stories--a virtual impossibility.

Chapter 8

The day that I met him, I knew I would always love him. He wasn't like the other farmhands who drifted in and out of Harrisville each year to plant and to harvest. Most of those fellows I had seen before, but he was a stranger--one somehow set apart from the others.

He walked into The Mercantile one early Tuesday afternoon with a group of the men from the farm south of town, and I walked in with my first lemon meringue pie for the day.

He looked at me and said, "Ma'am, I'd sure like a piece of that. It looks real good."

He made eye contact with me. So few customers looked right at me, knowing that I had no words. I guess they felt it rude to demand my participation in their world. Clearly, he had no idea I could offer little response. But when he asked, I did respond. I had to do it, so I just smiled. I sliced off the pie and looked up at him. He was beaming back at me.

"I haven't had a slice of pie for so long. My momma used to make them. She quit though. She just quit."

When he looked at me, he grinned again. For once, it didn't matter that I couldn't speak. I remember him leaving the store that Tuesday with the bright sunlight setting his frame aglow dancing across the silhouette of his shoulders. The bells on the door rang as it slammed shut, and he was gone, but I knew he would return.

He was a mystery. My father, Nathaniel, tried to find out where this young man was raised, who his family was. No one knew. It was like he just emerged into our world, like he stepped through a curtain onto a well-lit stage. To say others were interested in him was an understatement. A gentleman, so kind, so chivalrous and so sincere stood out brightly among the groups of crude, filthy workers migrating in and out of town. Folks hoped he'd stay. They prayed he'd marry their daughters and raise beautiful strawberry-blond babies.

I knew this man liked me best. I knew it even when the young ladies about town began making their purchases during the lunch hour when he arrived for pie.

He had been coming in every day for three weeks. Sitting at the counter, I would slice off an extra big piece, serve it with my eyes and a smile. Then, I would continue my work in the store. Most of the time, I simply dusted the shelves; sometimes, I rearranged items for sale. I would do whatever it took to keep me in the store while he was there, but at the same time, whatever it took to keep my secret. I watched him, studied him. He showed little interest in the ladies shopping. Sometimes, when I raised my eyes to peek at him, he was stealing a glance at me. I would look down immediately like he'd caught me in a lie.

Of course, my father caught onto this act, and I believe he felt I had a chance to win this man's heart because he didn't discourage the game I was playing with him. Surely, all fathers hope their daughters marry well. Although I'm convinced my father hoped I would simply marry, just marry.

He often said that, if I would only use the writing I was taught to express myself, then husbands would line up outside The Mercantile for me. It simply wasn't worth it to write. My father talked so much to me, to Lucinda, to my mother, to customers, to neighbors, and to animals. He even talked to the walls when he thought no one was there. If he had to write all his words down, I knew he would give it up himself...and quickly. I found it, at a young age, easier to simply listen and nod or listen and smile. My eyes gave way to a multitude of words. My voice did not, but I knew I heard more than my father. I understood people better than he did.

I knew this man could handle my silence because I had listened to him in the store. I watched him, too. He spoke very little, but what he said mattered. He tuned into emotions, read others' faces. One day, my father was pacing in the store. He was agitated, fidgeting. I knew it to be a result of mother's horrible ranting during the night.

The man said, "Why, Mr. Swanson, you act like you haven't slept a wink from worrying."

My father stopped his pacing and looked into the man's eyes.

"Did you peek in my windows last night, young man? I'd have never guessed that if I were you. I'd have guessed that I was worried about the price of flour or tobacco or maybe about marrying off my beautiful daughter but never that I'd been up all night. I'll tell you what though--you're right, son. You're absolutely right."

My father cackled, slapped the man on the back, and offered him a cigar.

The man politely refused.

The next day, when the man came in, he seemed so excitable, overwound. What was most strange was that he refused the pie I had cut and placed on the counter for him. I tried to be gracious, but my feelings were hurt.

He said, "Katerina, may I speak to your daddy please?"

He spoke my name so clearly, so beautifully.

"You sure can," my father said as he walked in through the front door. He had been sitting on the front porch. The man, the one I knew I would love, must have walked right past him.

"How can I help you, Eli?" my father asked.

"May I...um...speak to you privately, sir?"

Well, that was obviously the last of the conversation I was going to hear. It didn't matter though because, within five minutes, I knew what had been said.

My father came barreling in the kitchen and announced, "My darling Katerina, Mr. Eli Johnston will commence his courting for your dear, sweet heart this evening at 7:00 PM sharp. I suggest you change your frock, bathe in some of Lucinda's fancy rose water, and maybe pinch the rose into your cheeks a bit."

I remember this announcement like it was merely a minute ago. I was so happy and yet so frightened all at once. Never in my life did I dream of being courted by any man, much less one as handsome and kind as Eli Johnston, a man the wind seemed to have blown into town just for me.

Lucinda's Story

Chapter 1

*O*n the day I was born, my grandfather used the pages of a Bible to soak up Momma's blood. He claimed that the Lord would understand the necessity of it considering that was all he had. Momma delivered me inside an old barn out in the woods behind the town of High Hill. Grandfather prayed to his God as he lay the pages of Luke, Acts, Matthew, and Ephesians all over the dirt floor for Momma to lie on.

Two weeks to the day before I was born, the home where I was to be raised into womanhood burned to the ground. Some claimed it was an accident, but I knew better. The people in the little village of High Hill burned our house to the ground on purpose. They did it because they thought Momma was a witch.

She claimed to be a virgin and my conception to be immaculate, but that didn't make her a witch. People scoffed at her and my grandfather, too, for their peculiar ways.

Momma said she had visions. She claimed the eye of God dwelled in her mind and when she closed her eyes, she could see it, staring at her, directing her course. She declared me the new

Messiah, returned to the earth to save God's people. The eye, she said, told her this. Well, I was no Messiah, at least as far as I could tell, but I did have a powerful tongue and a demanding presence.

Momma brought me into this world as easy as you please, but that was about the only thing that came easy for Momma. With no man by her side but her aging father, our future looked bleak. But Momma, you see, believed in her God. She believed in the eye as well as the church in her body. She knew that glory and goodness would prevail. Not an hour after I was born, Momma pulled herself up off of the floor, and with the bloody pages sticking to her feet, she swaddled me in her under-skirts and told Grandfather that it was time to depart. Ignoring Grandfather's protests, Momma started walking.

They walked with little struggle deeper into the woods among the tall trees and the wispy grasses for what seemed like no time at all. Momma always said it felt like they were being pulled somewhere, like they were floating to their destination. A mile or two into the walk through the deeper part of the woods, there appeared a cabin as if it rose from the ground. The eye told Momma that this was her new home. Standing before this cabin, Momma claimed she really looked at me for the first time. She saw my fire-red crop of hair, touched my skin. I was her flesh and blood, God's messenger.

The cabin, although old and full of spiders' webs, was sturdy and safe, so Momma and Grandfather quickly took up house-keeping there, living off of the land by growing cucumbers, beans and potatoes. Momma would venture to town to barter vegetables for the finely colored fabrics that she stitched into dresses and frocks for me. Momma never dressed me plain. I wore red to match my hair and never a pattern in the fabric, neither a flower nor check, solid reds of every hue. Grandfather and Momma dressed in scraps and rags, but I was always adorned in glorious flaming color.

I spent my childhood wandering in those woods. I made chains of clover, blew the heads from shimmering, white dandelions, and nursed injured birds, bugs, and squirrels. Sometimes successful and sometimes not, I quickly learned the powerful force of the natural world. Momma taught me these things, and she showed me where God lived in the trees, in the air, and in my mind. She taught me to treasure all life with abandon.

My hair grew long, wild, and unruly, but never did my Momma cut it or restrain it. Strands flew wildly in the wind and drew up into tiny tendrils in the rain. Momma and I danced every night as the moon rose, spinning circles in the grass around the cabin and through the trees in the woods, laughing and singing, praising God for our happiness. My hair danced with me, and as I lay down to sleep, I wrapped it around me.

When I was about eight years old, Grandfather was weak. The eye told Momma he was to die soon, and I must become an adult. It was then that she began to teach me to read and write from the pages of the Bible. A gifted child, I excelled at my studies. By the time I was nine, I was writing my own poetry that Momma believed to be the word of the Lord.

Momma started taking me to High Hill with her to barter and purchase goods for our home each week. It was on one of my first trips to town that I understood what it meant to be Momma. High Hill consisted of a handful of homes, a church, a blacksmith, and a big, old store. Most folks lived on little plots of land outside the town boundaries. On Saturdays, when we always went to town, so it seemed did everyone else. Momma always brushed my flaming hair and adorned me in the glorious fabrics of fire before grabbing her basket full of goods to barter in town.

Next to the other girls walking with their mothers, I looked quite different. No one would speak to us or look at us directly. Wide gaps were made for us to pass. We were not accepted. Women would grab their children when we walked by them. One old man would drop to his knees to pray as we approached him outside the church door.

Momma would just squeeze my hand, lift her chin, and walk. I quickly learned to imitate her, made her strength my own. Unfortunately, holding our heads high with pride only marked us with the devil's stamp in the eyes of those people, but their eyes didn't matter to Momma.

By the time I turned thirteen, I had grown long and lean; I was considered beautiful in the eyes of many, but not by their words did I know this. Their eyes gave them away. Saturday mornings in town were filled with eyes staring at me in my blood-red frocks.

As years passed after the death of Grandfather, whose dying was hardly acknowledged by Momma, I learned to understand

Momma's acceptance of life's many circled paths. All things, she believed, happened at the hand of God. Grandfather's life needed no celebration, and his death deserved no sorrow. The eye prepared her for all things, and all things were perceived as leading to a higher Godly goodness. While the sorrow was great in my heart, Momma acknowledged no true emotions, only the will of the eye. Thus, when the stranger came out of the woods and into our clearing that cold winter day, it was no surprise Momma proclaimed him a messenger of God and invited him into the safety of our home.

His name was Manchester. His dark hair hung down on his face and and the base of his collar in greasy strands. His beard was bushy and looked like it had never been shaved, giving him the appearance of a wild animal. His brow was furrowed, and his skin was thick and leathery.

He claimed he had been traveling for going on two years from town to village and hunting in the woods around each one of them. He sold what he scavenged to local stores who were willing to buy wild pelts and meats.

"I been attacked once, by a big ole' bear," he claimed time and again. "Killed that sucker with my bare hands, but not before he darned near ripped my leg off."

Manchester was right about that. He walked with a steady limp giving his body an off-kilter appearance as if he were actually two people. Momma, who believed the bear to be the devil himself, never doubted whether his limp was a gift from a bear. Manchester had defeated evil, according to Momma. She claimed he walked in white light that surrounded his head and body like a halo.

I adored Momma with all my heart, but the day Manchester walked into our lives was the last day I spent with the mother I adored. The changes were like fluttering whispers. If you weren't listening, you never would have heard them. But Momma was all I had, and I knew her clear through to her bones.

It didn't take him long to catch onto the ideas Momma had in her head about him or to catch onto the eye in her mind. He soon blinded it. Then, he took her to her own bed. He told Momma that he was an angel sent to this world to wrap his wings of love around her and keep her from harm. They closed themselves off in that little bedroom hour after hour. Momma claimed she was in love with something holy. Manchester told Momma that the Lord wanted her to bear him a son. This son was to be the new Messiah.

Within three months of Manchester making a home for himself with Momma and me, she was pregnant. It wasn't that she said so to me; it was the shape of her breasts in her nightgown, the way she craved the wild meats that Manchester hunted in the woods, and the sickness that sweltered around her all July.

Sweat poured off of her as we worked in our garden. But that was when we did work, for Manchester and Momma still spent many hours alone together. Even when Momma objected, Manchester would tell her it was the will of God, and Momma would oblige him, every time. She was ragged and wilted most days, her hair a mess, and her eyes sunken in her skull. At night when it was time for moon dancing, she would simply drop to her knees and rock and pray under the stars, gone was her abandonment, her freedom, gone was Momma.

I woke to find her that August lying on the floor of the cabin in a pool of blood, Manchester nowhere to be found. The baby, or what there was of a baby, lay in the blood pooled around her. She was weeping with tears that shook her entire body and forced her chest to heave. The new Messiah was lost.

When Manchester, sweaty and filthy, returned from the woods that afternoon, he found Momma lying in bed and chanting over and over, 'Why hast thou forsaken me? Why hast thou forsaken me?"

I had handled Momma carefully all day. I had bathed her with heated, soapy water from the well and scrubbed the blood from her gown and the floor. I had washed her hair gently and pulled it up loosely in a bun away from her sallow face. I saw the wrinkle in her brow and the transparency of her eyes. I saw deep into her. I saw her truth. She believed. She knew she killed the Messiah.

I remembered Manchester's words that day like they were the first words he ever spoke, "You get on out of this bedroom, Lucy, I want to spend a little time with your mother."

The door met me, and I realized it may as well have been the door between Heaven and Hell.

With not a tear streaming down my face, I spent the rest of the day alone. I sat on the front porch and brushed my hair, combed it and fought it until a person would have thought my scalp would be raw and bleeding. My face grew flush and sweat trickled down my nose and beaded over my lip. By the time the sun went down, I had ravaged my hair; it lay in slick waves down my back and snuggled closely to my scalp. I could feel the weight of it, the burden of it. Not a word from the bedroom did I hear, not a word.

I slept on the planks of the porch that night, the heat of the cabin being unbearable. The wind moaned through the trees, and the night birds sang their mournful song. When sleep would not take me, I watched the path of the moon walking across the night sky. I begged to be delivered. I asked the Lord to kill Manchester, this angel of God, and I pled for mercy and forgiveness for even letting the request fall from my lips.

When I woke the next morning, the air was moist, and my body ached with stiffness. I felt a heaviness, and I rose to turn and see Manchester sitting behind me in the old rocking chair.

"Hello, there, sweet Lucy! Sure is hot out here, don't you think? Now don't you worry 'bout your Momma; she gonna be just fine, just fine indeed."

I never looked Manchester in the eye, not once in the few months he'd been with us. This time, I did look him straight in the eye.

"You aren't an angel!" I said with fire and brimstone in my mouth.

"Now, how you know that, little girl?"

I had nowhere to turn. My mind had failed me. My soul had taken over; my intuition was screaming loudly.

"Cause angels don't climb into bed with women. They don't make them bleed and cry. Angels don't do any of that. You aren't an angel. You are just some no good drifter who just happened upon our little house. You weren't sent from God. The devil sent you!" I screamed hysterically with rage.

Manchester didn't even move. He didn't even blink or seem to breathe.

"Well, what you gonna do 'bout that? Tell me. What you gonna do?"

He rose from his seat like a beast of Hell. He grabbed me by the hair of my head. His eyes were so close I could barely distinguish that he had two of them. His breath fogged into my face and covered my skin with filth.

"I'll tell you what you gonna do. You gonna do nothing. Absolutely nothing. Cause if you do, if you say anything to your Momma, I'll kill you both. You hear me. I'll kill you both. I am an angel, by God. I am."

He tossed me to the ground off the side of the porch.

"Now you go on and fetch some water from the well."

I turned around to walk away from the house toward the well, and I felt another pair of eyes upon me. Through the bedroom glass, I could see Momma's face peering out, watching us. Her eyes bore deeply into my own. She shed not a single tear.

I could sense him behind me as I made that walk to the well. The birds were silent that day, no happy song to sing. I heard his heavy footsteps behind me and felt a hand in the middle of my back. It pushed me, and I fell face first to the ground--the grass mingling with my hair that guarded my face from him. He was on me, just like that, without a word from him, without a scream from me. He threw my skirts up and ripped down my undergarments. I lay there in the grass without a God to pray to anymore. When he entered into me, I uttered no sound although I felt he had ripped me to pieces; one part of me would live and the other would die. I knew I would not come out of this whole.

"Pray to me, girl," he grunted. "I have come from God. I am your Lord to worship. I am your Savior."

I said nothing. My head, which was buried in hair and skirt and grass, was miles away in a place where Momma moon-danced, where she adorned me with color, where God was as soft as a fallen leaf or a baby bird or a flower petal. I was not here with this man on top of me. I was not here.

Chapter 2

*I*t took only a few months for Manchester to plant the seed in me. Nightly, he would come to me. I obliged him with not a word or a look. Momma knew. She knew...She did nothing.

He told me that Momma couldn't bring the new Messiah; she was too old. Momma believed him. She gave me to him as a sacrifice for some God I no longer knew. Manchester, however, was wrong. Momma was not too old. As my belly swelled, so did hers. I realized that Momma was with child, too. We were the same, trapped by a devil's seed.

Her pregnancy was ragged and weak. She rounded very little, and yet the weight of her body seemed to drag her further into the earth. I, however, was robust and full. My breast swelled for the unborn child that I carried inside me. While Manchester hunted for wild game and disappeared for days at a time, I worked myself hard in preparation for the births; Momma, too fragile, lay in bed most days, staring and searching for an eye that had left her. I canned vegetables and bartered

89

some of my cherished, red dresses in High Hill for blankets and supplies the babies would need.

Every time Manchester left, I hoped that he would not return, that he would lose his life, that he would meet up with another bear. Momma who prayed for his safe return smothered my hopes. Manchester arrived, and my water gushed out on the cabin floor.

My baby was born. He was a healthy boy with big blue eyes and a short, plump body. His hair flamed in colors of fire just like mine, and he took to my breast with ease. He was beautiful, and although he came to this world through violence and filth, I loved this child. I named him Eli.

Momma's birthing was not so easy. She struggled for hours and pushed for what seemed forever. Nothing came from her womb. She screamed in agony and bit down hard...but still, her womb would not release the child and end her anguish. Attending to her as best I could, I pushed on her stomach, lifted her up, nothing. Finally, ten hours after her water broke, she let out a terrifying scream and pushed forth a child: a girl, a lifeless girl. The child's little body was misshapen and missing what it needed for life. I felt sickened but thankful, considering my little Eli lying right next to me was healthy and strong. One of the deformed child's eyes was closed, and the other was open. I stared at her face. I reached down and closed the other eye. My mother lay in a pool of sweat and loss. Manchester forced himself into the room and demanded to see his child.

"She's dead," I said with hatred on my tongue.

I took Eli and left the room to nurse him.

Momma never said another word about that baby. Manchester buried her out in the backyard of our cabin with no stone or cross to mark her grave and no name by which to remember her.

Chapter 3

I soon realized that Momma hated me for the birthing of Eli. Even though Manchester still came to her nightly, her womb remained empty. She could produce no Messiah.

My Eli grew stronger; at six months, he was plump and contented. My milk was strong and plentiful. That was when Manchester went to town. He came back with a goat. In exchange, he took almost all of the vegetables that I had canned for the winter.

"This is for the boy," he said. "He don't need your milk no more."

My breasts filled with nourishment for little Eli, but I was denied.

Each time he needed to be fed, Manchester milked the goat, and Momma fed Eli by spoon, denying the babe my breast.

My breasts were painfully engorged with milk, and my love for this child was so great. I pleaded with Momma.

She said, "This is not your child, dear. You have become confused. He is our child. He is our new Savior."

In short time, I was being dragged through the woods toward the little town of Harrisville by Manchester who suddenly claimed to be my father. I knew he wasn't, but I also knew better than to say anything. As we approached the edge of the woods that opened up into the clearing behind Harrisville, my heart was dying for my son, and my breasts were aching.

"Say nothing of this to nobody," I heard him say, "or Eli will die and your Momma, too. Your baby is dead, got it? Your baby is dead. You say nothing and don't come looking for any of us. Or I swear I'll kill you all."

With the sun in my eyes, I saw the silhouette of a man waiting for us on the other side of the clearing. He held something in his arms, but the sun was on fire, and I couldn't see the baby Katerina whom he held up next to him, the child who soon took to my breast as if she were my own.

As we walked, I prayed that Momma would return to what was true. I prayed for death to descend upon Manchester. I prayed for these things earnestly, especially Manchester's death. I asked God to make it gruesome and did so without guilt. The bastard deserved to die.

Manchester and I stepped silently out of the woods as if we both knew the walk was something reverent, and something huge lay before us and behind us. When we reached him, the man who had been a silhouette merely introduced himself as Nathaniel Swanson. With strong hands, broad shoulders, and twinkling eyes, this Nathaniel was a true man even though I saw the fear of youth in him. I could tell that he had lived a lifetime already.

Manchester gave me to Nathaniel without a thought. When he squeezed my breast full of milk, I felt ashamed and ridiculed.

Nathaniel hardly seemed to react, for he so needed nourishment for his starving child. How could he know, or even care, that I was starving as well? I didn't know how I could go on without Eli, a child who filled me with love.

Manchester pushed me into Nathaniel and his baby.

"You take her. Don't even try to bring her back and keep your damn money. She ain't worth nothing to me."

Although Manchester shoved me into his chest, I wouldn't even look at Nathaniel. There was no trust in my heart for any man. I was worn and disheveled. The baby began squalling.

I walked with this new man through the field separating the woods from Harrisville, up the front steps, and into The Mercantile. I did so without uttering a single word. Nathaniel placed my old sack full of red garments outside the door of the room where I would sleep. Life began again.

Chapter 4

y milk was abundant, and although I felt love for the innocent child in my arms, I couldn't help but pretend that she was Eli, fat and gurgling up the sustenance I offered. As I nursed Katerina, I would daydream about Eli, growing and learning. I would think about him crawling in the tall grass, creating stories about the animals in the cabin yard, the squirrels, the rabbits, and the robins. I imagined him playing and dancing in the moonlight. All the while, I tried desperately to swallow the fear I had for his safety. He must survive. I prayed that he be spared, that Manchester would never be filled with violent schemes. I prayed this for Momma, too.

I had no idea where Katerina's mother was and no idea when Nathaniel would come upon me, but I knew that he would. At night, I pushed the dresser in front of my bedroom door. I slept lightly, partly because of the baby, but mostly because I feared Nathaniel. His eyes were lustful, and he often looked at me in the places a woman didn't like. I would catch him out of the corner of my eye. I knew.

One evening as Katerina lay sleeping in my arms, Nathaniel came to me. He fell at my knees weeping. These were hard, heavy tears for a man. Between sobs, he told me the story of his child, her mother, and himself. He had been innocent, easily swayed by an older woman; she had seduced him and tricked him into marrying her. The baby? He loved the child, knew she was his own blood, felt that in his heart. Beyond that, his heart was cold for the woman who had so little to give her own child.

I rose from the chair as Nathaniel rose from the floor.

"Your hair," he said, "is the most beautiful shade of red that I have ever seen. Oh, Lucinda, I have been without a woman for so long. I see the way you love my child. Could you not love me as well? Could you not find it in your heart?"

Nathaniel knew my answer before he even asked the question. He knew I could not love him. He knew that I could give my heart to no man. He knew I disliked him simply because he was a man. When he reached up to touch my face, I bowed my head and lowered my eyes. He would not see my eyes. The fire within them might give way to desire for something I could not have. It was not Nathaniel I wanted but instead my sweet Eli. Too proud to trust Nathaniel and too scared to tell him the truth, I allowed Nathaniel to believe my son was born dead. Not to do so would surely mean certain death for Eli and Momma. I could not risk allowing myself to truly care for this man, for that would be weakness. Women make mistakes when weak with love. If anything remained of what Momma taught me, this was it. Nathaniel would try to rescue my child and Momma. He would do it out of love for me. That was the method of men. They go out of their way to rescue women, save them from their lives, and then they seduce them, suck the life out of them.

I saw how Manchester did this to my once powerful mother, a woman so centered and grounded in her faith. He ripped her heart from her chest, poked out the eye of the Lord, and stripped her of her firstborn child. I could never return to the cabin. It had become a devil's pit from which no one would escape alive. I knew this, so I kept my secrets and my feelings to myself. It gave me power in a situation where I had nothing more than weakness. Eli, above everyone else, had to live.

I noticed early on that something wasn't right about Katerina. When she was hungry, her face wrinkled up to cry, but her voice let forth nothing. She didn't coo or even whimper like little Eli did. No, this child was silent like she held some dark secret deep within her. At times, I feared her dead, for even her breath in sleep seemed silent. Sometimes, I would wake the beautiful child just to be sure that she hadn't been taken. It's a wonder she rested at all that first year, for I soon noticed Nathaniel woke her from slumber, too.

Caring for Katerina was far from easy. Even when she cried, no sounds of agony came forth. One had only her eyes and her tears. I hardly left her alone in a room. She was with me always. Rarely did I allow her face to be removed from my view. I believed that the child sensed this. As she grew, she was always underfoot. She was constantly looking at me. Her eyes were so round and so dark. A person would have thought any number of secrets could be drowning in there, but, in truth, Katerina held no secrets within her. All was written plainly in her eyes.

When my love for Katerina grew, it was nothing less than bittersweet. Every joy she brought to my heart was accompanied by visions of Eli. She was, however, the core of my world. She was what held me steady each day because she needed what I had to give. She forced me to stay within myself while others would have gone mad when faced with my losses.

Nathaniel was more felt than actually seen by me. I avoided his gaze simply because I did not want him to read my eyes, not that I didn't want to read his. I was curious about this man who was hardly more than a boy. I could feel his eyes from across the room. His eyes were penetrating and deep; he followed me with his child. He burned through to my soul, with wave after wave of adoration. I had the man's heart within my grip, but I always chose to release it, every time. I gave him no hope, only blazing coldness.

Still, Nathaniel persisted during those first few months of our life together. He brought me flowers from the garden, red ribbons, and candy. I loved the candy best. I would look down when he arrived with it, and he would place it near wherever I was. I would never touch it in his presence, but when he left, I would race to it. He never said a word to me about it. I felt like an animal whose owner attempted to seduce it with treats to bend its wild will. I was tempted by something as simple as a child's treat. At times, it worked even though I knew the destruction this type of desire could bring with it.

Nathaniel must have been on the verge of madness those first few days and months. Of course, Katerina thrived. Of course, I had love to give her, but all we both gave Nathaniel was silence, innocent and painful. So we lived together with our demons until Nathaniel's wife rose up to face the silence with blood curdling screams deep in the belly of the night.

Chapter 5

I had been in the house about two weeks before I realized the wife was also with us. I had asked no questions, so how could I know? Strange, in that time, she made no noise at all. The women of the house banded together in silence until the screaming suddenly began. In my passionate unwillingness to talk to Nathaniel, I simply assumed that Katerina's mother left him to care for the baby alone. Nathaniel said that he could not love this woman who had no nourishment for Katerina; therefore, she must have abandoned them. I was wrong.

Nathaniel had been mysterious however. Frequently, he disappeared from the store, putting up a quick sign in the window to call attention to his absence for a spell. During these times, I noticed little of what he did. As the disappearances continued and happened more frequently, I decided to follow him. I realized he was coming and going in and out of the doorway toward the end of the hall upstairs. It was always a closed door. I held little interest for anything other than the child, so I had yet to feel any curiosity as to what lay behind it. That began to change when I noticed Nathaniel's comings and goings related to whatever lay behind the dark, shadowy door. It seemed so far removed from all of the activity in the home.

On this particular night, I pinned up my hair high on my head. Pieces and curls dripped over the top of the pins. My hair seemingly belonged to a woman. As I placed the last pin into my hair, the first screams began. At first, it was a dull moaning, but it progressed to rhythmic grunting and breathing. Then, the screams slammed into the ceilings and the walls; they shot through doorways and rattled the windowpanes.

I quickly walked down the long hallway toward the shadowy door. The screaming lived just beyond it, trapped inside its walls. I reached out for the knob, but Nathaniel opened the door from the other direction. Inside lay the woman whom I would soon know as Esther, wife of Nathaniel. She was swollen and fleshy, writhing on the bed. Her naked body filled my eyes with shame.

"Please," she panted.

Nathaniel responded with, "Go to sleep now, Esther."

He looked me directly in the eyes. I saw him for the first time. He was raw and utterly alone. His eyes begged for something that he had no words to express. He quietly closed the door.

"Good night, Lucinda," he muttered. His eyes evading mine.

"Good night, Nathaniel," I whispered.

These were my first words to the man. Nathaniel slipped by me and down the hall to his own room. He was unaware that

I had even spoken, completely unaware. Silence again slipped over the night and muffled the secrets within our walls.

Nathaniel spoke little of his wife and took care of her himself. He entered her room but three times each day staying longer as the day dwindled. At sundown, she would begin. I never rose from my bed, but I could imagine her thrashing about in her bed. What struck me odd was her silence during the day. I assumed this was so because she fought the night--and her demons--until the wee hours of the morning. As a result, I rarely received the gift of a good night's sleep.

Katerina had no trouble with slumber, and I feared she was deaf when she was tiny, but as she grew, it was clear she was not. When I called her name, she would turn her head toward me. She was sometimes smiling and sometimes not, but always with those eyes that bared your soul.

Chapter 6

*A*s the weeks passed, I hurt Nathaniel every day. I hurt him with the words I would not speak and the love I would not offer. I rejected him completely. I felt like a person torn into two pieces. I presented outwardly a countenance of pride, anger, and contempt while I hid inwardly a heart full of sorrow. Always I saw Eli in Katerina's face. Every milestone she passed was a milestone for little Eli...if he were still alive. My Eli, the Savior, kept my hope alive.

Sleep continued to be a hard fought trial. Esther screamed and thrashed nightly, and still Nathaniel spoke nothing of it, not a word. I began to wonder if I might enter her room during the day to help out. Maybe it would calm her, and sleep would come to all. I didn't speak to Nathaniel about my idea in any way; I simply opened Esther's door and entered her room. The darkness of it filled me with despair. Even in the bright light of day, it was night in there. She was almost always in her bed, a virtual invalid although nothing seemed to physically hold her in the room. Her body had not abandoned her. It was her mind that disowned her, leaving her trapped in her room each day.

She talked little and stared at me often, but not with anger. She seemed so empty and broken. She was not old, but she felt old, broken and brittle. I began to sit with her daily.

Over a period of weeks and months, her trust in me grew. She let me bathe her and bring her food. Her words were only about her Savior and the light, always about the light. This seemed so very strange to me considering the darkness of her chamber.

Nathaniel caught onto my willingness to sit with his wife, and he stayed in the store more frequently during the day. A routine established for us with little spoken of it. I spent the daylight hours in and out of the room taking care of Esther and Katerina, and he spent his evenings when the store closed in the room with Esther. I was her day, and he was her night.

Never did we discuss bringing Katerina to her. It seemed unsafe but also unimportant. Esther appeared unaware of the existence of the child, unaware of the existence of anything really. She saw the room she lived in as her world, and her sickness consumed her. She dwelled in thoughts of this mysterious light that she claimed was with her. I saw no light, only deep, dingy shadows.

She spoke in riddles of madness. There would be only brief moments of lucidness. During this time, what she said made sense but was not real. She recalled little from the past, just kept talking about her Savior and the light over and over and over again. At times, she mumbled, writhing as if in pain, talking in ways only she could understand. It was as if she were possessed by a demon.

I never questioned Nathaniel about her nightly tirades. What was I to do? She was his wife, the mother of the child. All he could do was care for her until she left this world. His destiny was tied to this tiny room with Esther.

To escape, he came to me for love I would never return and prayed for words from a daughter who would never speak.

Chapter 7

By the time Kat was five, Nathaniel and I had established a routine. We were not a family by any means although we both shared a great love for the girl. She had become my daughter, too. Eli faded into a hole in my heart that would never mend. I missed Momma, but alive or not, her spirit was dead. Because my mother hadn't come for me, I knew the eye was no longer with her. She surely possessed no power. The mother I knew would have bundled up Eli and escaped long before now. There were times when I thought of returning to the cabin, but what would I find there? Somehow, it seemed better to remain hopeful than to discover the truth. Better a chance for Eli to live without me than a chance to die with me.

In the five years I lived in the house, Katerina grew, flourished, and played with abandon. Esther's wailing at night became as regular as the moon or stars. I still pushed my dresser in front of my door each evening, and Kat slept in the same room with me. I had done this since she was so little that she surely thought nothing of it. Nathaniel had to stay away from me.

Not that I hadn't begun speaking to him, I had. It was about six months after I had been in the house. I was bold in my demands of him, pushing and testing his devotion, but giving nothing in return other than a meal and a mother for his child.

He worked hard to please me with gifts--a cameo, a looking glass and brush, beautiful fabrics. All these things I took. He even hired Spinster DuPree to clean our home and to wash our linens and clothing. Profits from the store were slight, but better than most fared in Harrisville. By the other's standards, Nathaniel was wealthy, and I was a freeloader. No matter to me, my responsibilities lay within Kat's eyes. I had to reach in there somehow. If she could hear and she could see, she could learn. I convinced myself that this was my purpose in life, the reason for my mother, the reason for Eli, the reason for every loss I owned. I was to teach Kat to communicate. Little did I recognize that she already knew how.

Katerina's education came long before the age of five. As with any other child I suppose, I merely pointed to an object and named it. There was nothing wrong with the child's hearing. In fact, it was far more acute than regular folks. Kat heard everything from the sweet whispers of prayers or the random words one speaks to herself while cooking. Even if she were not in a room, she was drawn magnetically to the words within it. She absorbed them but never released her own.

I believed that if I taught her to recognize letters, then words with pictures, I could teach her to flood Nathaniel and me with the pent-up thoughts of her young life. I realized quickly that to teach Kat letters was ridiculous. Instead, I went straight to words matched with pictures or objects. Her difficulty lay in the written word. Kat clearly recognized a spoon. She could also retrieve one from the drawer when it was requested. All I had to do was connect the object with the word. I began with obvious things, things that she needed or wanted but could not request. We started with a cup.

And so her education went for hour upon hour and season upon season until the day Esther died. That day, our young Kat learned what it meant to be a woman.

I always doubted Nathaniel. There was just something within him, something cursed. But he loved Katerina, and he also took good care of us all, including Esther. By all appearances, most considered him an honorable fellow. He was nice enough, and he'd given up on any affection from me; instead, he kept a respectable distance letting me run the house while he managed the store.

It was an agreeable situation. Katerina thrived, but for every year she grew stronger, my hopes of reuniting with Eli faded. Sometimes, I would peer out over the fields to the edge of the woods convinced I had seen something moving, a person, perhaps my son. I'm sure others would have returned to look for Eli, but the risk of death for Momma and Eli would be too great. Never once did I let fall from my lips that I was afraid, too cowardly to go back to find my own truth--that Eli and Momma were dead. It was almost better to go on without knowing. Manchester's darkness went to the core. He was capable of the murder he threatened. Regardless as each year passed, I became closer to my dear Kat. How could I leave her with an insane recluse for a mother and a cursed father to care for her? Women need to be raised by women.

Chapter 8

That morning I had risen earlier than usual. I had learned to sleep through Esther's wailing, but this night, it had been unending. Confident that Nathaniel was already awake, I walked down the stairs to the kitchen. I could see the early light pushing through the crack under the doorway to the store, but something about this light was different. It beckoned me, seeped through my pores, drifted into my eyes, and encircled my head. It lured me through the door. I was in The Mercantile before I grasped that I had even entered.

I walked forward as quietly as a I could, but with each step the old wooden floor let forth a groan of pain. Other than the floor though, not a sound could be heard. It was eerie. I headed toward the entrance of the store. I felt uncomfortable, without my bearings. I was waiting for something, looking for anything, and struggling to contain my fear.

Without warning, what I was drawn to lay before me. It was Esther. She was sprawled on the floor with a baby between her bare legs. Her white nightgown was pink with her own blood. The baby's face was covered with the gown. At her feet stood Katerina.

The room was alit in a strange shade of orange muffled by dark storm clouds encroaching.

It was the gun that I saw after that. Suddenly, everything moved as if walking through deep, deep water. I heard my own voice's warped echoes; it was screaming. "No! Please, no!"

I felt the store shake all the way to Hell. Esther's body jerked and gave way to nothing, just stillness.

I felt my heart pounding in my own head. Suddenly, I heard Nathaniel's panicked, ragged breathing.

He fell to his knees and crawled to Esther. He held her limp body up to his. Tears streamed down through the crevices in his face. Our eyes met, and I knew. In the blinding morning light, I knew.

Chapter 9

As the years since Esther's death passed by, I could carry the burden of the truth inside no longer. I told Nathaniel...I told that man I had enough of his falsehood, of the pretense. I swore that I would tell anyone who would listen to the truth, what I had witnessed with my own eyes, what Katerina also knew as truth. I swore I would release us all from the web that entrapped us, a web spun by Nathaniel.

We deserved to live in truth, in the light of reality. Katerina lived this lie because she loved her father, but the lie constrained her. Elizabeth's life held but fragments of reality, leaving nothing but a festering soul. The truth would come out. I would tell it.

As I approached Elizabeth sitting at the kitchen table with Katerina, Nathaniel stepped in front of me.

"The man, Manchester, who disowned you...he's alive and well. He's living in those woods with his ole lady and a young fella."

My face did not betray my fear or my hope.

"I could let him know you're looking to reunite the family. I could do that, you know." He smiled sweetly.

Elizabeth and Katerina heard him well, and they would recognize this as kindness. I had to think quickly. This temptation was actually an opportunity to end the lives of my mother and my son.

I whispered disgustedly under my breath, "I don't want to reunite with that man. So, the answer is no. I do not wish for you to do that. That won't help you anyway. I'm telling Elizabeth today."

"I think you misunderstand me, Lucinda. I'm not asking you what you want. I'm telling you what I'm going to do if you don't keep quiet. You pack up your things and leave today. My love for Katerina and Elizabeth is greater than any love I still have for you. You've given me nothing after all these years, so nothing is what you're going to get. Leave today. If you don't, Lucinda, there's going to be a family reunion, and it's going to be yours."

The thoughts I'd had about Nathaniel over the years burst forth uncontrollably in my head...how I'd noticed his shoulders the day I'd met him outside the woods, how I loved the peppermints he gave me in hopes of gaining my heart. I pondered how we had passed each other at Esther's threshold day after day and year after year. But always I had held him back, kept myself from him, refused to even offer true friendship.

Nathaniel and the girls were all that was normal in my world, and in a split second, he ripped it from me. He was uprooting me from anything ordinary and safe. He was letting go, but not to free me. Oh no, he was letting go of me in order to hold tight to all who were dearest to him.

Without a word more, I packed up my belongings in a satchel, walked out into the daylight, and headed down the road away from his home and away from the woods where my heart had always resided.

I wore my dress of flaming red. My head faced forward, and I looked straight into the horizon, holding myself with dignity. Whether anyone saw me or Nathaniel noticed my absence mattered so little. The survival of my son mattered most, and by Nathaniel's account, he was alive.

I walked away from Nathaniel, Katerina, and Elizabeth to save Eli. And though my heart yearned for him, I knew that it just couldn't be. I had lost one family to save another again. Alone, I walked down the dusty, windswept road. I knew my son was alive in those woods behind me.

Elizabeth's Story

1914

The Mercantile was quiet. Grandpa was sitting behind the counter with a cigar dripping out of his mouth, staring out the window, and willing the heat away. I looked at him closely and saw the crevices in the corners of his eyes, the hills across his brow. He looked his age and maybe then some. His hair was bright silver, thick and wavy. He swore he'd never lost a hair in his whole life; problem with that was that he had an abundance. His hair grew bushy and curly in his brow line and twirled and swirled out the holes of his ears. In a lot of ways, Grandpa looked more animal than human; his voice gave him away every time.

"Get on over here, Sis; I am gonna put you to work. Climb up on that stool and take down those old cans of tomatoes. They need a dusting, and you look just like the young lady to do it."

I did what he said to do, just like always. But in my mind, I didn't feel like it. Climbing up and down in a big ole skirt dusting tomato jars on the hottest day of the year didn't seem like the thing to do.

I made it to the top of the stool when she walked in the door of The Mercantile. She was an attractive woman with wild hair strung up loosely in a knot. The wrinkles around her eyes framed them and only made her more attractive. She was one of those people who, when you looked at her, you really couldn't say why she was pretty, not really, just something about her made it so. That's the kind of pretty she was. I was so caught up in the woman that I didn't even see her approach my grandfather. All the same, across the store by the counter she stood, and the heat was radiating off the both of them.

"Hello, Nathaniel," said the woman with a wide, gapped-tooth smile that gave her away.

It'd been five years, and I had been but nine when she left. And yet, she was standing there with that all-consuming fire in her eyes. The "Hello, Nathaniel" had rolled of her tongue spewing flames so hot that Grandpa could not seem to stand in one place for fear of getting burned. Grandpa said nothing, didn't move, didn't even seem to blink. The only change in him was his mouth, wide open, shocked, his pink tongue hanging behind his teeth like he hadn't had a drink of water in weeks.

I hadn't ever heard anyone call Grandpa by his first name the way Lucinda did. It had an air to it, a quality that made a person squirm. It was grinding like she was trying to smash something into him, make him bleed. No one ever said Lucinda was a nice gal; everyone knew she wasn't. There was just this softness way down deep that kept a person attracted to her even when you didn't like her.

"I was just passing through. I thought I'd stop and see an old friend," said Lucinda. "I'm staying at the Shady Oak Inn."

Of course, I was still standing up high on that stool looking down on them. Lucinda's eyes reached up to mine. They were deep green, piercing and small, but gentle all the same.

"Who's that pretty gal up there on that stool? Why is that my baby Elizabeth? Come on down here and give your Lucinda a hug, a big one."

Grandpa turned and looked up at me with ice in his eyes. I'd never seen such a thing out of him before. I couldn't move.

Suddenly, he spoke, "Lucinda, I thought I told you not to come back."

"Come on down here, little girl. Come see me, sweet Elizabeth. Come see me," called Lucinda.

I was frozen cold to that stool. I could barely get a breath much less move. Grandpa moved himself between Lucinda and me. Lucinda's fire met Grandpa's icy glare. I had never seen Grandpa so full of anger. It welled up in him, made his eyes glaze over inside his head.

I decided to speak. I said, "It's fine. Grandpa. I'm not afraid of Lucinda. I remember her."

Grandpa turned to looked up at me high on that stool. He reached up with his hand and helped me down from it.

"Lucinda!" he blared. "I need to ask you to leave my store and never return!"

Again, Lucinda ignored him. I felt backed into a wall that wasn't there. The air felt heavy and thick. I was trapped in one spot. The room that had been spinning stopped cold.

"Why, Nathaniel, now you know that isn't possible. That baby doesn't belong to Katerina. I'm here to take her with me for good. Katerina deserves a chance to live her own life, and Elizabeth deserves a chance to know the truth."

"Katerina's my momma," I uttered, more to convince myself than to be heard.

My eyes lowered to the floor. Lucinda seemed to have lost her mind since she'd been gone.

"Get out of my store!" Grandpa roared, his ears full of color. He grabbed her arm.

Lucinda bellowed, "Let go of my arm, mister. I'll leave when I'm ready. Listen here, Nathaniel, that little girl standing before you is coming with me. Poor Esther's gone, and you threw me out once without that child, but this time you aren't going to do it. Remember this. I will be back for this girl, and there isn't a thing that you can do about it, you hear, and you know why there's nothing you can do, Nathaniel? Don't you? Don't you know, Nathaniel? Now let go of my arm."

Lucinda just kept chanting her anthem all the way to the door of Grandpa's store. "I will be back, and that girl will be leaving with me."

She said, "Nathaniel, you aren't worth a dime, and you know it. Fess up to your so-called granddaughter here. Tell her the truth, Nathaniel. Tell her the truth! Tell her what you sold your soul for, Nathaniel."

The little bell on the door was ringing and jerking as Lucinda fought with herself to stay or leave the store.

Funny how, in a moment of crisis, a person tends to remember a speck of dust on a counter near an old familiar hand, the way the mole on a cheek twitched with anger when the owner spoke, or the way someone's eyes blinked and blinked again. It's funny how the little details create a bigger picture, little details that never utter a sound, just sit there waiting for a person to notice. And isn't it funny how we always notice them, always.

After about an hour of silence since Lucinda left the store, Grandpa spoke, "Where's your Momma?"

When I said I didn't know, he sent me to look for her. I wanted to find her earlier but was afraid to leave Grandpa, afraid to do anything that might set him off. He seemed so angry, so full of fury, that I was fearful of him for the first time in my life. I had no idea what Lucinda was talking about, but it must have held some truth for Grandpa because his anger sure smelled a lot like fear. It smelled like the kind of fear a person cooked up over a long, long time, like it had just been stewing in his gut for years and years.

Momma was nowhere to be found for an hour after I started looking. The oven was cool, and the sink was empty. The backyard was cleared of branches, and the weeds had all been pulled from the morning glories; all of Momma's usual paths had already been walked. Just when I had given up hope and was walking in the side door to tell Grandpa that I couldn't find her, she drifted in the front door of The Mercantile like a ghost. Her hair, which usually hung long and loose, lay in matted curls around her face; her eyes were sunken, swollen, as if she'd cried the day away. Momma's lips were full, red, and parched. She needed water. Grandpa just stood there, staring at his daughter, saying nothing. A person could just tell when Grandpa was thinking, and he was thinking hard now.

"Where you been, Little Missy?" he said to Momma. "Does no good to run from the truth now, does it? Guess I need to learn that. Guess we all better learn that lesson real good before someone else teaches it to us. Powerful hard lesson to learn though, must say. Powerful hard lesson."

For the next couple of days, Grandpa didn't really address me at all except normal requests.

"My, those flowers out back need a watering. Get out there and do that for me now, girl...Get on in the kitchen and fire up that stove for your Momma...Wheats comin' in, and the fellas will be mighty hungry pretty soon...Go on up to bed now, you hear me? A young lady needs to gets some good sleep if she wants to make good babies some day...Getcha going."

Never, never did Lucinda come to his lips; never did he tell me one of his stories or even look me in the eye. He spent the days in the store, staring out the dusty front glass, smoking cigars, and waiting.

I had been feeling so mixed up that I hid from myself. I refused to think of Momma in the field with that man or Lucinda's fury in the store that day. Grandpa and I walked around our world like we weren't even really there, and nothing was real.

Nobody seemed to much care what I did as long as they knew where I was. I felt my family's eyes upon me all the time, but they only saw my presence in the room, the house, the store, the garden; they weren't seeing me. They didn't know what I was pondering, not at all. What truth did I deserve to know?

One week from the day that Lucinda walked out of the store, she walked back in. The wind was circling that day around the old dirt road in front of the store like a tornado. When I was real young, I'd see those wind funnels and think they really were tornadoes. I'd run and hide under the kitchen table until they passed by. As I aged, I'd sit and watch them and wonder what it would be like to spin round and round in a circle of dust until it dropped me some place new, some strange place I'd never been.

Like I said, the wind was rolling down the road pulling up leaves and sticks in its path and twisting them into the sky when she walked into the store. I had just settled onto my stool in the back to read my Bible.

I glanced up from my reading when the door opened because the wind caught hold of it and banged it against the opposite wall. I jumped because I had spent most of my time since Lucinda's return on edge.

Her eyes landed on mine. She glided right past Grandpa who was spittering and sputtering as he stood at the counter. She walked right past all the canned goods, the baking goods, the cleaning supplies, and stopped right in front of me.

She was hardly the Lucinda I'd witnessed the week before; she was changed somehow. She wore a glowing red dress, and her hair was sloping every which way.

"About time you learned the truth anyway, just about time," Lucinda whispered. "People living a lie around this place. It's time for that to end."

There are times when so many things happen so quickly that it is impossible to even comprehend them.

Lucinda's words slid out to me in mere moments while Grandpa seemed to run in slow motion behind her. There was no way he could arrive in time to stop her from speaking to me. Whether he heard her, I did not know, but her words lay like vomit everywhere. I couldn't breathe, couldn't hear, couldn't see. What she said crashed into my heart and shattered it into tiny pieces. It could not be true; it simply could not be, but here she stood claiming the unthinkable. I suddenly sickened. I felt the pain that truth can bring in every inch of my body.

The Bible slid out of my hands. It came tumbling down beneath my feet. As I fell to retrieve it, a note was stuck in a crack of the floorboard. The book lay open to pages of hand-written script that I had not noticed before this moment. How could I have not seen them before now?

"Elizabeth, you're going to be just fine," Lucinda was mouthing to me, her head bent down in my face so that her lips seemed to protrude forth, exaggerated.

Strange thing was that I don't remember Grandpa saying a word. His mouth was moving, but nothing was coming out of it, nothing I could hear anyway. He was just holding the note he had picked up and looking at me and then the book and then Lucinda. He seemed like a child. He was helpless. His whole world just fell to the ground beneath his feet. He handed the folded note to me as I rose. My gaze fell upon the book. Lucinda noticed it, too.

She looked directly at Grandpa. She smiled at him; to me, it was unreadable. She took my arm and guided me out of the store. I went with her. I was walking, but I didn't know how. I went out of The Mercantile without a fight.

I emerged from the darkness of the store with its creaky, old wooden floors that suffocated the noise of the voices within it. I stepped into the light of the day and onto the main road that ran by its entrance. With Lucinda holding me gently by the arm, I looked up. I had to place my other hand above my eyes to block the blinding sun. On the road stood Katerina and the man called Eli. They were waiting for me. My family was waiting just for me with the wind dancing around them blowing us far, far away from here.

Esther's Story

I was Esther. I don't recall their names. I remember the face of only the young girl, the one with the eyes. The baby, well, I don't know what to say about her. I can't see her face, just have the memory of giving birth to her on the floor of the store.

I had gone down to the store from my bedroom because that is what the light told me to do.

"Go to the store, Esther; deliver the child at your father's feet."

So I did. The pain started as the orange light of morning began to peek through my small bedroom window. I felt compelled to go to the store as if by force. I was no longer in control of my body as it began to bring life forth. With all my effort, I drug myself down the hallway and the stairs and into the musty store. When I could walk no further, I lay down right where I stood. The pain filled every inch of my body as the baby forced itself out of me. I pushed but three times lying there on the floor, pushed with everything I could find within myself. I forced the child out into the world.

I had the baby, who had no face, on the floor in the dark except it wasn't at anyone's feet. No one was there. No one at all, except me and that baby girl. Don't know how long I lay there, could have been hours, could have been days. I didn't think about that baby. I just let it lie in our blood still attached to my body. I didn't think about how it needed me or why it whimpered. I only thought about how it got in my belly in the first place.

I didn't think Nathaniel understood that Lucinda lived in the house with us. Nathaniel, me, and the girl with the eyes. Lucinda was invisible to everyone in the house but me, so I told her my secret--how a big white light was the daddy of the baby with no face.

I don't remember Lucinda saying much but, "What baby with no face?" and "You need rest, Esther."

I guess Lucinda didn't know that the baby with no face was coming.

In the morning, the sun began to rise skimming through the store windows. It filled the room with light, with so much light, that I thought it was lifting me from the floor, calling me to rise, but I could not. Then, there was nothing but Nathaniel. I lay at his feet. He held his gun. He pointed the barrel straight at me. His aim did not waiver.

His eyes glowed, and his mouth was moving. I could not understand, but he wasn't talking to me. No, he wasn't; he was talking to Lucinda. How could that be?

I tried to tell him, "God sent us this child. Look, she has no face. Look, she came from a beam of light. It was the light that sent her."

I heard it first. It was an explosion that shook me to the core. As the light dimmed to nothing, puddles of thick blood flooded across the floor flowing between the toes of the one with the eyes. My firstborn, standing above me, was all I could see.

Lucinda lived on without me in my house raising the one with the eyes and the no-face baby even though she was invisible. From my grave, I knew more of her than the living do. I saw Nathaniel and Lucinda talking the day the baby came in the store. I understood the heat of Lucinda's will. Why, how else could she blow enough into her body to make it visible to Nathaniel? It was sheer holy will.

One day, her body will melt back into particles of sand that blow like dust off of the storefront porch and tumble on down the road...back to where she came from. No one really knew Lucinda but me, and I am dead.

They say that the dead tell no tales, but that is a lie. The one with the eyes didn't speak, and she was one of the living. She had sin's curse cutting her throat. Funny how her name won't come to my lips. She was the one whose throat was cinched tight. She pretended to be the mother of the one with no face because she was scared not to be. She was not her mother though, and that secret burned deep inside her. This was no one's fault but mine.

See, I'm just going to tell you. She let my daddy do it, my momma I mean. My daddy walked into the room every night, and the light from the hall would set his head aglow like he was Jesus. Sometimes, when my daddy was on me with my eyes squeezed tight, I'd pretend he was Jesus because everything's alright if you're with something holy. Pretty soon, I just decided that the hallway light was the glorious light of the Lord himself. I was with Jesus the whole time my daddy lay with me. I just wasn't there anymore. Then, Nathaniel came along at just the right time.

That didn't explain much now, did it? You see, the light came to me even after my daddy died. As I lay in that bed over the store, the glow of it from the hall haloed his head as he came to me. Every night, he came. I lived for it. I never wanted to get out of that bed. I might miss his coming. I hoped that he would come in broad daylight and take me home with him, but he never did. It was Lucinda who came in the daylight. Lucinda would sit by my bed, help me change gowns, comb my hair.

At night, she disappeared into dust as my savior arrived. When he left, I would scream and beg, roll on the floor, beat the walls. I guess it was because of my thinking. I wanted him to come back, and all there'd be was old Nathaniel sitting there half asleep in a chair trying to keep me from hurting myself. My savior wouldn't take me. If I didn't settle down quickly enough, Nathaniel would strap me to the bed; by then, my clothing would be strewn all over, and my body would be prickled with sweat.

When your mind stops working, things that bother others seem perfectly fine. I didn't care if Nathaniel saw my fleshy body, smelled the sweat from it, or watched my breasts smash into his chest as he threw me down to the bed. I didn't feel sorry for it. I was already gone.

You'd think the Lord would be right by my side, but he isn't. I cannot find him even though I think I'm in his mansion full of nothing but light, just like the light that shone from the hallway. I thought when I got here, he'd meet me, and we'd finally be happy together. I don't understand why I cannot find him. Where could he be?

Did I tell you Lucinda was invisible? She was. She had powers, I am sure of it. When Jesus came, Lucinda had left me for the day. That's how I knew she couldn't be seen. I've never seen her in the same place with anyone but me, and that included the Lord. She said she'd take care of things around the house, but how did she do that? Nathaniel spoke nothing of her when I was calm in my bed, strapped and sedated. I can't think about it too much. It doesn't matter. I am just waiting because my savior's coming.

Lucinda lived on without me. She raised the one with the eyes and my no-face baby, but no one could really see her. I was the only one, and even on earth from my bed, I knew her more than the others did.

I cannot see or feel the presence of anything holy, not like I did from my bed above the store all of the years. Each night, the presence came before me, lay upon me, filled me with light year after year. This glorious light came floating through the doorway to my room as night fell. It ravaged me and left me spent and exhausted. The one with no eyes came from this light. I was her passage to this place, but I could never see her face, never hear her breathing. She was my offspring, mine along with the Lord, but I could not touch her or help her or speak to her. I did not exist in her world. In her world, another filled my space, leaving no room for me but just enough room for an untruth to stand on solid ground.

I know what I saw, and I know what I believe. One might believe my truth to be a lie; after all, my mind has been suffering for many years. But, I swear on my own grave that the truth is what I carry. It is not, however, what others carried. They held falsehoods in their hearts, and it festered and rotted inside them. The truth has become muddy--the lines blurry. I don't recall their names.

They've disappeared into the wind, blowing away and drifting on without me.